Just this one time to ~~~~~~~~ one time to love
him, fully and completely. This one time to grasp a life's
worth of happiness.

"Love me, Griffydd," she pleaded fervently. "Love me
now. Tonight."

"We will be married," he promised as he reached out
for her.

She smiled at this honorable man who would not take
what she was offering without some kind of promise
between them.

"I will always be yours," she replied softly, and truthfully,
hoping it would be enough.

It had to be, for there was no more she could say.

"I love you with all my heart, wife-to-be," he murmured,
pressing feather-light kisses upon her forehead and
cheeks. "I am yours forever."

"Shh," she hushed, afraid that if he called her "wife"
again she would start to weep. "Later. We will speak of
these things later."

Even though she knew full well that there could be no
later for them.

All they would ever have was this one time.

Dear Reader,

This holiday season, we've selected books that are sure to warm your heart—all with heroes who redefine the phrase "the gift of giving." Since 1992, Margaret Moore has written seventeen full-length historicals for Harlequin and two short stories, and will soon publish her first historical for Avon Books, *A Scoundrel's Kiss*. Look for it around Valentine's Day. Critics have described her as "a master storyteller," and "a genius of the genre." In *A Warrior's Passion,* the ninth book in her medieval WARRIOR SERIES, a young woman is forced into an unwanted betrothal before the man she truly loves—and whose child she carries—can claim her as his wife. Don't miss this exciting story!

Linda Castle returns with the long-awaited sequel to *Fearless Hearts, Territorial Bride,* in which a cowgirl and an Eastern rogue must put their love to the test when she is thrown from a horse and seriously injured. *The Shielded Heart* by rising talent Sharon Schulze is the gripping tale of a warrior who learns to accept his special psychic gift as he teaches an enamel artisan about life and love.

Rounding out the month is *Harrigan's Bride* by award-winning author Cheryl Reavis, who also writes contemporary romances for Silhouette. Here, Thomas Harrigan returns from the Civil War to marry the bedridden, abandoned daughter of his late godmother. It's great!

Whatever your tastes in reading, you'll be sure to find a romantic journey back to the past between the covers of a Harlequin Historical® novel.

Sincerely,

Tracy Farrell
Senior Editor

Please address questions and book requests to:
Harlequin Reader Service
U.S.: 3010 Walden Ave., P.O. Box 1325, Buffalo, NY 14269
Canadian: P.O. Box 609, Fort Erie, Ont. L2A 5X3

Margaret Moore

A Warrior's Passion

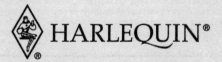

HARLEQUIN®

TORONTO • NEW YORK • LONDON
AMSTERDAM • PARIS • SYDNEY • HAMBURG
STOCKHOLM • ATHENS • TOKYO • MILAN • MADRID
PRAGUE • WARSAW • BUDAPEST • AUCKLAND

ISBN 0-373-29040-3

A WARRIOR'S PASSION

Books by Margaret Moore

Harlequin Historicals

* Warrior Series
† The Viking Series
Δ In-line Christmas Collection
‡ Most Unsuitable...

Harlequin Books

Mistletoe Marriages
"Christmas in the Valley"

MARGARET MOORE

confesses that her first "crush" was Errol Flynn. The second was "Mr. Spock." She thinks that explains why her heroes tend to be either charming rogues or lean, inscrutable tough guys.

Margaret lives in Scarborough, Ontario, with her husband, two children and two cats. She used to sew and read for reasons other than research.

Chapter One

Seona MacMurdoch sniffled and wiped her dripping nose with the back of her hand. Clutching her thin woolen shawl tighter around her shoulders, she raised her head, squinting in the drizzle, and looked up at the slate-gray sky.

No sign of sunlight and, inside the stone hall beside her, not a sound that would give any notion of why her father had summoned her.

Unfortunately, there was nothing to be done but wait until the chieftain called for her or sent one of his men to fetch her inside, provided he even remembered that, at one time this morning, he had wanted her.

Breathing in the scent of the wet earth beneath her leather-covered feet and the soaked thatch above her head, she wiped her damp face again and sighed with resignation. Then she leaned back against the wall, the movement setting the iron keys tied to the plain belt around her thin waist jangling. Her gaze roved over the wooden wall of her father's fortress to the scraggy hills surrounding the bay, the thin, dark green of them obscured by the rain. From where she stood, she could look out the open gate of the fortress to the harbor, where the trading ships of her father's fleet rocked in the bay.

Although these were heavier, larger vessels than longships, the sleek hulls and curved prows gave evidence of Diarmad MacMurdoch's Norse heritage. He and his people were Gall-Gaidheal whose forebears were both Scots and Norsemen here on the northwest coast of Britain.

His other ships—his longships—were moored elsewhere, out of sight of the village and any traders who might come to visit Dunloch.

"Seona!"

She jumped at the sound of her father's bellowing voice. It echoed off the stone walls of the hall as if he had called from inside a cave.

Before she could obey her father's order, however, the warriors of Diarmad MacMurdoch's council filled the entrance, then filed out past her.

This was to be a private meeting? She shivered and told herself it was from the damp chill of the air of late spring, not the fear that she had done something wrong.

Clad in their voluminous yellow shirts called *leine chroich* whose color showed their wealth and status, cloaked against the cold and wet by *brats,* long, woven pieces of cloth they tucked into wide leather belts so that they hung to their naked knees like skirts, their shins wrapped with *cuarans* of deerskin held in place by thongs, the warriors paid little heed to their chieftain's daughter as they passed her.

It was not that they didn't notice her, standing there holding her cloak closed over her loose woolen gown without so much as a bronze pin for adornment, or would not be aware that the chieftain was awaiting her entrance. By their aloof behavior, they only emulated Diarmad MacMurdoch. He often went weeks without speaking one word to Seona, or seeming to realize she still lived and breathed.

Not that Seona wanted any of her father's warriors to pay her particular notice. Around the time she had come of an age to be married, she had decided she would prefer to be ignored by the lot of them.

Nor had she any wish to see the dread in their eyes should fierce Diarmad MacMurdoch take it into his head to forge a family tie with one of them. She would rather remain a useless spinster, as her father so often described her.

Did any one of them ever wonder how she felt about the prospect of becoming his wife? Did they believe her blind to the curl of their lips when they glanced at her? Did they think her blushing face and awkward manner born in her, rather than engendered by the knowledge that all men thought her ugly and graceless?

"Seona!" her father bellowed again.

She obediently entered the cavernous hall. There

were no windows, and the only ventilation came from the covered door and a hole in the thatched roof. A peat fire smoldered in the central hearth, and its lingering smoke added to the obscurity.

Despite the lack of light, she knew where her father would be, so she advanced confidently, as a blind person does in a familiar room.

Wrapped in his black bear robe, the chieftain of Dunloch sat on a bench at the far end of the hall, his back against the wall. A neck band of silver glinted dully as he stared at her with stern disapproval, his dark eyes glaring beneath brows as black as the fur surrounding him. His beard and hair, now shot through with gray, had once been that dark, too. Nevertheless, he was a dangerous man yet, despite his age, as his enemies would aver, whether in combat or in trade.

"You wanted me, Father?" Seona asked as she took off her cloak and shook out what water she could.

"I never wanted a daughter," her father growled.

Seona made no answer as she folded her wet garment over her arm. This announcement did not surprise her; indeed, she had heard the same sentiment expressed many times before.

Her father leaned forward with a grunt. "You are the scrawniest woman I have ever seen."

Seona carefully laid her cloak on a nearby bench. "I know," she answered evenly, wondering how long this preliminary criticism would last.

Many a time he chided her for her pale face, odd-colored hair, staring eyes, too-large mouth, too thin body and too full lips. He claimed that she took after her mother's family, which had only ever produced one woman worth looking at, the one Diarmad had taken for wife.

"Lucky for you, I may have use for you yet."

"What task would you set me?" Seona inquired, thinking he was going to speak to her regarding provisions for his ships or food for his men.

His scowl deepened as he leaned forward again and fixed his beady black eyes on her. "We're going to have an important visitor. From Wales he is, the son of a very powerful, rich baron. He's coming to conclude a trade agreement."

Seona nodded, thinking she knew what her father wanted. "I will see that quarters are prepared for him and his men."

"He brings no men."

Seona's eyes widened a little, and then she smiled. Her chores would be much easier if the man came without a band of warriors.

"I've sent one of my ships to bring him here, and his father sends him alone to show his trust in me."

Seona fought hard to keep any skepticism from her face. Her father's reputation was not one to generate much trust among his trading partners.

Not that Diarmad MacMurdoch ever broke his word or harmed any ally. No, he was trustworthy as far as that went. But no one who made a bargain with him ever felt they got quite a fair deal, and in that, they were absolutely right.

"Very well, Father," Seona said, turning to leave. "I will insure that all is ready."

"There is more!"

Seona turned back to face her stern parent again. "Yes, Father?"

"You are to see that he is kept...happy...while he is with us."

Her eyes narrowed as she regarded her father with a shrewdness his allies would have recognized. It did not ease her suspicions that her father did not meet her gaze. "What is it you would have me do?"

As the silence stretched between them, her instinct became a certainty and anger began to build in her breast.

"What would you have me do?" she repeated.

When he still did not answer, she squared her slender shoulders. "You would pander your own daughter for the sake of trade? I suppose I should be surprised that you have never made such a proposal before. However, I am not so ugly or desperate for a man's touch that I will act a whore!"

"Did I tell you to sleep with the man?" her father retorted. "What have I asked of you except to see that my guest is made welcome?"

"I will see that his quarters are prepared as befits a valued ally," she said firmly. "I will see that we have good food and drink to serve him—but no other needs will *I* fulfil."

Her father shrugged his shoulders, and the scowl on his face was suspiciously like a pout. "You are not getting any younger, Seona," he remarked, "and you've never been a beauty. You could do a lot worse than Griffydd DeLanyea. His father's a powerful man, part Norman, too. Maybe if you—"

"Went to his bed, he would marry me?" She made no effort to hide her disgusted skepticism. "Father, who is it always says no man will buy what he can taste for free?" She wrapped her arms about herself. "Besides, I am not for sale, like furs or gold."

Diarmad MacMurdoch regarded his only daughter coldly. "What is every marriage but a bargain? This would be no different. I've fed you and clothed you all these years, letting you live like a leech on my skin. It is time someone else took you."

"You will offer me up like damaged goods?"

"If I must."

"I am your daughter!"

"So what of that? I have sons to succeed me and fight for me. What will you ever do? Even if you marry, you will need a dowry—and where is that to come from, eh, but *my* purse?"

"I did not ask to be born!"

"No, and I did not ask for you, either!"

"I will not shame myself—"

Her father suddenly rose up like a wrathful spirit. "Do not speak of shame to me, girl! Have I not lived in shame these twenty years, aye, since the day you were born? Shame to have a daughter first! Shame that she was a weak, skinny thing! Shame that she was ugly! Shame that no man would have her, no matter how much I offered!''

Every word was like the sting of the lash to Seona, even if she had heard it all before.

Except the last. *That* was something new, and devastating.

''How much?'' she asked in a whisper as cold as the wind from the hills in winter.

Now it was his turn to look startled. ''Eh?''

''How much were you willing to pay someone to marry me?''

Scowling, he wrapped his robe about him and shrugged one shoulder morosely. ''It matters not.''

''It does to me. I would know my worth.''

''Five hundred pieces of silver.''

And still no man wanted her! Dismay washed over her—and yet she would not give in to it, or to her father, either, just because no man of any wealth or consequence would take the bribe, for only to such would her father extend the offer. Otherwise, he would keep her by his side to run his household.

So it did not matter that a man of *his* choosing would not take her, she thought as she lifted her too-pointed chin.

''You should be glad I am here,'' she said, ''and that you have me to run your household. Am I not cheaper to keep than another wife would be? She might demand some notice from you, or lacking that, material goods to keep her happy.''

She ran a scornful gaze over her father, the chieftain of his clan, the leader of his people, the trader all men respected. Then she slowly and deliberately untied the ring of keys from her belt and held them straight out. "I learned better than to ask you for anything long ago. Would you have these back?"

"No!" her father growled.

"Then I will do my duty—but no more, not for you or any man!"

"Daughter—!"

"Servant," she interrupted. "Little more than slave."

"A servant would do her master's bidding without an argument! A slave would know her place. By God, I should have drowned you like the runt of the litter."

She regarded him steadily. "Aye, Father, perhaps you should have, but it is too late for that now. And alas for you, I am not a servant."

With that, Seona turned on her heel and marched out.

Holding to the curved prow to steady himself in the bow of Diarmad MacMurdoch's vessel, Griffydd DeLanyea drew in a deep breath of the salty air and gazed at the craggy hills of this godforsaken country. While Wales had hills and mountains aplenty, it also contained trees and lush valleys. All he could see here in the north was rock touched with a bit of green. Perhaps when the ship drew closer, the land would not look so barren.

Thank the Lord he didn't have to live in the place, though. All he had to do was reach an agreement with Diarmad MacMurdoch, whose ships sailed all around Britain, the Isle of Man and Ireland, as well as north to the land of the Norsemen and Danes, and south to the Normans and even the Moors.

Griffydd's father's sheep produced some of the finest wool in Wales, and a lot of it. The baron's tenants had also discovered silver in the hills near their castle of Craig Fawr. These two commodities would bring the family much wealth, if they could get it to several markets. Baron DeLanyea knew almost nothing about the sea and ships; better, he had told his son, to strike a bargain with a man who did and pay for his expertise.

"Yet have a care, my son," his father had cautioned, "for a tricky man is Diarmad MacMurdoch. He will rant and rave and try to wear you down with his dramatics. That is why I send you, Griffydd. You have the patience to wear *him* down, with silence."

As the ship turned toward the shore, Griffydd smiled sardonically at the memory of his father's final words. Patience? Oh, yes, that he had—as well as the ability to overlook emotional outbursts, which he considered childish indulgence.

Indeed, he had always thought any display of extreme emotion rather distasteful and weak, even as a child. Like his mother, he could hide his feelings.

Not like his cousin and foster brother, Dylan. Dylan's every emotion flew across his face and shone out of his eyes. There was nothing secretive about him, and no solemnity, either. He seemed to fall in love with a different woman every day of the week and clearly thought this something to brag about. He had already fathered three bastards that they knew of, and Dylan's purse was perpetually empty supporting them and their mothers.

Being Welsh, of course, there was no shame to him or the women or the children—and yet no glory, either.

In Griffydd's eyes, Dylan's boisterous behavior was nothing more than rank foolishness and vanity. To be sure, Griffydd was no virgin, but he made no declarations of passionate, everlasting love to any woman. Why would he, when he never felt anything except the pleasure of physical union? No emotion had ever affected him the way the bards claimed love should. That such love existed he knew—his own parents were proof of that—but he mercifully had never felt the uncontrollable desire, the fierce longing that made all else unimportant, or the despair if the woman did not reciprocate.

The captain of the ship barked an order. Suddenly the crew jumped into motion.

They all had the look of the worst of Vikings about them, with long, tangled hair, thick, filthy beards and clothes that smelled as if their wearers had been living in them uninterrupted for the past ten years.

As the men lowered the square sail and prepared to out oars, the ship rounded a rocky point, exposing a sheltered bay. On one side of the bay on the top of a bluff stood a round stone tower that had obviously fallen into disrepair.

Inside the bay, several midsized vessels used for transport and trade sat at anchor. He could not see one longship, the low, dragon-prowed Norse warships all of Britain feared.

The captain pointed at the cluster of buildings now visible beyond the wharf at the edge of the bay. "Dunloch," he called to Griffydd, who acknowledged his verification with a nod.

At the man's next command, the oars slid out into the water. At his signal, the men began to pull in unison and, more surprisingly, sing.

At least Griffydd supposed that's what they were supposed to be doing, for they started chanting rhythmically.

The reason became clear: it was to keep the men rowing in unison, the oars dipping and rising in time to the song.

As Griffydd hummed the tune, which was not difficult to learn, his shrewd, gray-eyed gaze swept over the village, noting the number of stone buildings, the wooden wall of the fortress on a slight rise beyond, the activity on the right side of the bay that bespoke both the building and repair of sailing vessels, the fish drying on the beach, and the women and children working and playing there. Smaller vessels were beside a wooden pier stretching out into the water, or drawn up on the rocky shore.

Dunloch seemed a very prosperous place, and Griffydd would remember that when Diarmad complained of the harsh winter, as he surely would.

The captain came to stand beside Griffydd. ''You sing well,'' he remarked, speaking the language that was common among men on the coast of Britain, a traders' amalgamation of Gaelic, Norse and Celtic. ''Must be the Welsh in you.''

''Perhaps.''

The man heaved a tremendous sigh. ''A poor village, I'm afraid,'' he said mournfully, gazing out over the water toward Dunloch. ''It was a very harsh winter.''

Stifling a wry smile, Griffydd nodded his head, giving the man a sidelong glance. ''Harsh in Wales, too, it was.''

''Oh, aye?''

Griffydd nodded. ''There seems to be no lack of fish on the shore.''

The captain cleared his throat and ran a brown, brawny hand through his thick red beard. ''That's the way of it here. Good fish one day, no fish for ten.''

''A pity is that.''

''Aye,'' the captain agreed.

''Tell me, are the chieftain's sons in the village?''

A wary and yet relieved look came to the captain's eyes. ''No.''

Griffydd was glad to hear it, and he could understand the man's response. Diarmad had six strapping, obstreperous sons who were known to treat everyone with arrogant contempt. They commanded their own small fleets, quartered out of six villages within a day's sail of Dunloch. A wise plan to give them each their own village, Baron DeLanyea thought it, otherwise whelps like that would be at each other's throats constantly.

A cry went up from a watchman on a rock near the shore, which was answered by the captain. Another call sounded in the village, and now Griffydd could make out more clearly the people on the shore.

And they would be able to see him. With that in mind, he made his way to his chest in the stern to don his mail, hauberk, finest cloak, best brooch and valuable sword.

As he did so, Griffydd DeLanyea felt no sense of foreboding, or fear that he would not be successful in his quest for a good rate for the transportation of his father's goods. He truly believed that he would conclude this business and be safely home in no more than a fortnight.

Such is the folly of young men.

Chapter Two

A s the ship slowly drifted into its place beside the wharf, the left-hand side closest to shore, Griffydd scrutinized the men assembled there.

The stocky one in the center wearing the fur robe would be Diarmad. Not only was he in the position of leadership, there could be no mistaking the man, to go by his father's description.

The collective expressions of the men clustered around him indicated something less than joy at Griffydd's arrival.

This did not surprise the young Welshman. Alliances, whether political or mercantile, were not something to be taken lightly. The political affected trade, and trade affected politics, so no transaction of the magnitude of the agreement Griffydd was going to attempt to negotiate could be a simple business.

Men in the bow and stern leaped from the ship to the wharf, carrying ropes to tie the vessel in place.

As Griffydd jumped nimbly to the land, Diarmad

MacMurdoch stepped forward with open arms to embrace him and give him the kiss of greeting.

"Welcome!" the chieftain of Dunloch cried heartily. "Welcome to Dunloch! My hall is yours!"

As Diarmad drew back, Griffydd managed not to wrinkle his nose at the man's powerful stench. Instead, he acknowledged the greeting and gravely said, "I thank you for your kind words, Diarmad. My father, Baron DeLanyea, sends his greetings and some gifts from Craig Fawr."

The old man's eyes gleamed with pleasure and, Griffydd thought, greed. "I thank him! He is well, I trust?"

"Very."

"Glad to hear it! A fine man—a fine fighter! The Baron DeLanyea was on the Crusade!" the chieftain declared, apparently for the benefit of the men around him. "Nearly killed, he was, but the heathens couldn't do it, although they took his eye. Isn't that right, young DeLanyea?"

"Yes," Griffydd acknowledged, his body slowly adjusting to the solid, unswaying land.

"And your mother? She is well?"

Griffydd nodded. "Yes."

"Good, good!" Diarmad cried, throwing his arm about Griffydd like an overly friendly bear, which was, Griffydd realized, what was familiar about his smell. "To the hall then, for some ale."

Griffydd had no choice but to agree, for Diarmad's beastlike grip did not loosen. The chieftain led his guest along a wide street through the village to the fortress.

The Welshman felt the eyes of the villagers on him, but he paid that no mind. Instead, he concentrated on what he saw—the smithy, with more than one man busily at work, the well-built houses of stone and thatch, barns, storehouses, wooden outbuildings and even the muck heaps, which could easily tell a man how many horses were kept. Dogs ran barking around them, the largest obviously Diarmad's hound, for a word from the chieftain brought the brute impressively to heel.

"Fine mail you've got there, DeLanyea," Diarmad noted in a conversational tone. "That sword's a marvel, too. Must have been a prosperous year."

"The mail and sword were gifts from my father's friends when I was knighted," Griffydd explained truthfully. "The cloak and brooch, as well."

"Generous friends you've got."

"And powerful at court, some of them."

Diarmad gave him a sidelong glance but said nothing.

Griffydd sighed rather melodramatically. "As you know, the king has raised our taxes again, and of course, the winter was harsh."

There was a nearly imperceptible pause before Diarmad responded. "Oh, aye?"

"I heard it was bad here, too," Griffydd continued evenly.

"So it was, so it was!" Diarmad muttered.

By now, they had reached the tall, wooden wall of the fortress. As they went through the gate, Griffydd took note of the stables, the longhouses, the well— but everything inside the fortress palled beside the enormous stone hall in the center. Although the hall was smaller than his father's, it was impressive nonetheless, larger and longer than any building of the Gall-Gaidheal Griffydd had ever seen before.

Diarmad strode toward the building and proudly gestured for Griffydd to enter. "Well, here we are! Not so fine as your father's hall, I know, but fine enough for a poor man like me."

If Diarmad's poor, I'm a girl, Griffydd thought sarcastically as one of Diarmad's men, a dark-haired, sullen fellow, hurried forward to hold open the door.

Griffydd strode into the building, and suddenly felt as if he were in a cavern. There were no windows, and the sod-and-thatch roof gave the air an earthy smell. Smoke drifted toward a single hole above, with much of it lingering in the room lit by oil lamps and rushlights stuck in sconces in the wall. The lamps burned whale oil, if Griffydd's nose was any guide. A roaring fire blazed in the central hearth, providing more illumination, as well as welcome warmth after the chill of the air. Benches and tables ringed the hearth, drinking horns and trenchers already in place.

A sudden movement to Griffydd's right caught his eye and he swiftly turned to see a young woman rising from a stool in the corner. She wore a pale brown, rough woolen gown of simple cut. It fell loosely from a curved, unembellished neckline to the floor, although a plain belt hung about her hips and made the full dress blouse. Long, red-gold hair of luxuriant thickness reached to her waist.

Then, with one long-fingered hand, she slowly brushed her amazing hair away from her elfin face and looked at him, her dark eyes large, and their expression one he had never seen before—half defiant pride, half yearning vulnerability.

And totally compelling. As she was.

In that moment, it was as if the breath had left his lungs and his heart had ceased to beat. Then his heart came to vibrant life, thudding with a rapid drumbeat that surely had to be audible.

The woman did not speak or move, but regarded him steadily, her lips parted as if she would speak.

He waited, not breathing, for her to utter a single word.

Then Diarmad shoved his unwelcome way past Griffydd and broke the spell. "Seona!" he barked.

The young woman stepped forward and rose up on her toes to press a light kiss of greeting upon Griffydd's cheek, the sensation like the touch of a feather tip. She smelled of grass and sea air, a perfume of natural purity that pleased him far more than the costliest unguent from the farthest land in the East.

He had been kissed before, of course, but this gentle caress seemed to make his blood burn beyond anything even the most experienced and passionate of lovers had ever made him feel.

"This is Seona," Diarmad announced beside him. "Seona, this is Sir Griffydd DeLanyea of Craig Fawr."

As Griffydd bowed to her, a powerful surge of longing flowed through him and a wild thought sprang into his mind. Had Diarmad set her to wait here because she was to be Griffydd's servant—and whatever else he wanted—while he was in this village?

Such things had happened before when Griffydd had traveled on his father's business. Always he had refused the "hospitality," recognizing it for a tactic intended to distract him.

This time, however…this time, he decided without hesitation, he would accept.

"I am happy to meet you, Seona," he said, and with a gentleness that surprised even himself.

Then Griffydd DeLanyea did something even more unusual.

He smiled.

"Seona is my daughter," Diarmad declared with a proud and happy grin.

Diarmad's *daughter?* Griffydd's eyes widened with disbelief. This delicate woman with the bewitching eyes and hair such as he had never seen or imagined was the offspring of loud, brawny Diarmad Mac-Murdoch? He could more easily believe she was a faerie changeling.

Then he realized that wily old Diarmad was watching him closely, and Griffydd's smile dissipated like mist in the valley when the sun rose.

Of course, Griffydd thought with more anger than he had felt in many a day. A canny devil like Diarmad would use any ploy in negotiations, including setting his lovely, intriguing daughter to bewitch a man.

He had to be bewitched. No woman had ever made him feel as she had, and on first sight, too.

He had heard that these Gall-Gaidheals were only partly Christian and the other part pagan still.

A shiver ran through Griffydd as he turned away, suddenly aware that his task here might be more difficult than he had assumed, and Diarmad far more clever than he had anticipated.

Seona stared after Griffydd DeLanyea as he strode toward the bench at the end of the hall to take his seat beside her father.

She had thought to find the Welsh nobleman a short, squat, dark man, for weren't the Welsh all short and dark? Instead, she beheld a tall, gray-eyed warrior with doe-brown, shoulder-length hair that brushed broad, muscular shoulders. The complexion of his angular face was sun browned and his cheeks were ruddy from the sea breeze. His nose was remarkably straight, his jaw strong like the rest of him. He was well dressed in gleaming mail, black hauberk and a black cloak that swirled about his long legs when he moved.

Those things she had noted when he had first entered the hall and they had been surprising enough.

Then he had looked at her with his grave, gray eyes. What she had seen there had made her heart beat like the rapid movement of a bird's wings and filled her with a strange thrill such as she had never felt before.

What had she seen there? Approval, certainly, and that was rare enough. Admiration, she thought. Perhaps even desire.

In all her life, no man had ever really looked at her as if he thought her worthy of his interest beyond asking for food or drink.

As their guest drew off his cloak and took his seat to her father's right, the place of honor for a respected guest, she instantly recalled the sensation of the stubble of his cheek against her mouth, the sea-spray scent of his skin—and the yearning that had blossomed within her.

Most surprising of all, perhaps, was her sudden realization that if her father made his outrageous request of her again, here and now, she would eagerly agree.

Indeed, she more than half suspected if her father proposed a marriage with the Welshman, she would accept him on the spot.

Unfortunately, whatever expression had been in Griffydd DeLanyea's eyes, it had died when he found out who she was.

Why?

Perhaps he kept his smiles for serving maids, who

would be more procurable and appropriate bed companions than the daughter of his host.

Maybe he was playing a game. Perhaps her own astonishing desire had been too evident. He was a handsome man. He must be used to women's admiration. It was not so incredible that he might think to toy with her, encouraging or dismissing her as whim or strategy suggested.

Her jaw clenched as she told herself that if Griffydd DeLanyea had been truly canny, like her father, he would not have altered a whit when he found out who she was. He would have done his utmost to win her to his side, and so take advantage of her loneliness and anger at her father....

He could not know about that, of course. He was no mind reader, to reach into the recesses of her heart and understand her feelings, no matter how he looked at her with those iron-gray eyes.

Which meant she must and would subdue this wild excitement coursing through her, this sudden burning desire for a man she had only just met.

Yet she could not prevent herself from imagining what might have happened between them if she had not been Diarmad's daughter, but a maidservant.

Her body throbbed as her imagination envisioned— indeed, almost physically felt—being in his strong arms, his powerful hands and fingers caressing her body as he kissed her passionately.

The men of her father's council began to take their places, interrupting her ridiculous flight of fancy. As her father introduced them to Griffydd DeLanyea one by one, the Welshman completely ignored her.

No matter. She was used to that, was she not?

"Seona!" her father barked, making her jump.

Griffydd DeLanyea had said her name softly, in a way she had never heard before. Gently. Like a caress.

She grabbed the carafe of wine on the table nearby and hurried forward as other women entered with food and ale for those who preferred that beverage. Around her, her father's men spoke in low mutters and cast wary glances at their guest.

Not all of them welcomed an alliance with the Welsh, she knew. Some, like her father's oldest comrade, Eodan, would not question his plans. Others, like the religious Iosag, would look for signs from God as to whom they should choose as allies.

Then there were those such as Naoghas, a sullen, dark-haired fellow Seona had never liked, who would rather ally themselves with the Scots. Naoghas and his friends traced their forebears to the royal house of the Scots—or so they claimed—regardless of any influx of northern blood. They favored only compacts with Scots, and no one else.

As for her father, Seona knew he would unite himself to whoever offered the most profit.

She reached the head table and her fingers trembled as she began to pour the wine into the Welshman's drinking horn. She bit her lip, trying to gain control of herself, fearful that her father would denounce her clumsiness if she spilled any of the costly beverage and even more fearful of meeting their guest's steadfast, unnerving gaze.

"So, I hear that your sister has wed," her father said to DeLanyea.

Seona couldn't help listening as their guest responded in his deep, musical voice. "Aye, a year past."

"To the brother-in-law of Baron Etienne DeGuerre, too," her father noted. "A fine alliance for your family."

Seona moved on to her father's drinking horn.

"There is that, but it was a love match, too."

"Oh, aye!" her father answered with a sarcastic chuckle. "A love match that joins your family to one of the most powerful men in England!"

Startled by her father's blunt insolence, Seona jostled the carafe. Some of the wine spilled onto the table. Blushing with embarrassment, she quickly set down the container and wiped the spill with the hem of her skirt.

When she finished, she raised her eyes to see her father glowering at her while Griffydd DeLanyea's face betrayed absolutely nothing as he raised his drinking horn and drank the strong wine.

Then he set down the vessel and matter-of-factly said, "If Rhiannon was not in love with him, the marriage would not have taken place, even if Frechette were the heir to the throne."

"Oh, come now, man!" Diarmad protested as Seona hurried away. "Your father would—"

"Never use his child to further his own ambitions," their guest replied, still in that same prosaic tone, although he directed a pointed glance at Seona, then his host. "Unlike many men."

Seona flushed with humiliation and her hands clutched the handle of the carafe until her knuckles went white.

She knew what Griffydd DeLanyea was implying and she wanted nothing more than to repeat the same assertions she had made to her father: she would not be used as chattel for his bartering.

Yet while she could find the strength to speak her mind to her father when they were alone, here in the hall, before his men and their guest, she dare not.

Instead, she subdued her embarrassment and shame as best she could, and silently continued to do her duty.

Because there was nothing else to be done.

Griffydd tried not to notice Seona MacMurdoch's blushing face. It was more important that Diarmad realize Griffydd was aware the man might be trying to use his daughter as bait.

Therefore, Griffydd commanded himself, he would continue to ignore her, as he had been attempting to do since he had been told who she was. He had a responsibility to his father, and that he would fulfil, despite distracting young women.

All this talk of marriage hinted at one of Diarmad's plans. No doubt he had discovered that Griffydd was not married, or even betrothed. The cunning Gall-Gaidheal was probably hoping to seal any bargain between himself and the DeLanyeas with a wedding.

He would soon realize Griffydd was not easily trapped by feminine lures, no matter how tempting.

With such thoughts in his mind, he was glad he had been unable to see Seona's limb when she raised her skirt to wipe the tiny slop of wine. Nor had he paid any heed to the way the tip of her tongue touched her lip as she poured his wine. He would take no notice of her coy reluctance to look at him. He would not be drawn in by her alluring tricks, although his blood fired at the sight of her.

Forcing himself to concentrate on his host, Griffydd regarded Diarmad with a pointed look intended to let the chieftain know he felt insulted by his remarks but had magnanimously decided to overlook the insinuations, and for that, Diarmad should be grateful.

"Love and marriage are not something I care to discuss," he said evenly.

"So we won't!" Diarmad agreed with a chortle and an answering expression that told Griffydd his underlying meaning had been comprehended.

The chieftain turned his attention to the thick venison stew, redolent of leeks, set before him, swiping at the gravy with a hunk of flat barley bread.

What had prompted his host to scoff at the reason

for his sister's marriage? Griffydd pondered as he, too, sampled the excellent stew.

Perhaps Diarmad was trying to discover how quickly his guest angered.

In which case, he should have learned that Griffydd DeLanyea's ire was slow to arouse. Very slow, because that anger, once produced, burned long and bright, like the sun high above the desert.

As for other emotions that might be aroused, Griffydd mused, he would regulate them. He was in command of himself. He was not like Dylan, with his lovers and his children and his tempestuous, childish outbursts.

He would concentrate on the task at hand and forget enchanting young women with hair he would like to bury his hands in.

While ostensibly enjoying a drink of the wine, Griffydd's gaze swept around the crowded room filled with burly, bearded men.

How much did they know of their chieftain's schemes?

Griffydd could well believe that Diarmad would tell no one exactly what he planned: he was the kind of man to enjoy keeping the power of such secrets to himself. He couldn't be betrayed that way, either.

What of Seona, whose very name fascinated him?

Undoubtedly it would be better to think of her as a canny conspirator, at least for now. That way, he could control his wayward emotions regarding her.

He must control them.

"I confess my father was surprised that you seemed so amenable to a trade agreement," he remarked, determined to speak of other things. "He feared you would not wish to be associated with any save your own people."

"My own people?" Diarmad asked.

"The Gall-Gaidheal."

"Why would I set a limit on who I trade with, or whose goods I carry for profit?" Diarmad replied lightly.

"Especially when there is already to be an alliance between your family and the chieftain of Clan Ruari," Griffydd replied, naming a powerful group of Gall-Gaidheal. "I understand your eldest son is betrothed to his daughter."

"You seem to know much of my business, young DeLanyea," his host replied, eyeing Griffydd over his drinking horn.

"I also know that chieftain claims the throne of the king of the Scots."

"Show me a man, whether Scots or Gall-Gaidheal, who doesn't think he has a claim on the Scottish throne," Diarmad answered with another grin.

"I have never heard that said of you," Griffydd noted. *Although your daughter has the dignity of a queen.*

Diarmad threw back his head and laughed. "No, I do not make any such claim. My father's father was a Norse jarl and Haakon, the king of Norway, has dominion over me."

"Nevertheless, your son's marriage is not a love match, I take it, and it ties to you an important clan."

Again Diarmad laughed. "No, it is no love match. Nor is it a threat to you. His bride's father spends too much time thinking about the throne of the Scots instead of trade, but that's all he does—think. Set your mind at rest, DeLanyea, and tell your father that my sons and I, and all our allies, will steer away from your coast once we come to an agreement."

"He will be glad to hear it."

"As to the marriage itself, Corcadail could do a good deal worse, and not much better." Diarmad fixed his beady eyes on Griffydd as a sturdy wench set down a haunch of venison before them. "The same could be said of the man who weds my daughter."

"I am sure she will make a fine wife," Griffydd replied flatly. Then, because he could not help himself, he said, "I am rather surprised she is not already wed."

"I have been waiting for the right man," Diarmad answered. "How is it you have not married? You look of an age to have a wife and children long since. I already had Seona and two sons by the time I was about your age."

Griffydd shrugged his shoulders and raised his voice to be heard over Diarmad's warriors who, having refreshed themselves with food and drink, were growing loud in their conversations. "I see no need for haste in such matters."

"And I suppose you already have some sons. I have heard it said you Welsh don't care if your bairns come before a wedding or not."

Griffydd regarded his host steadily. "In that you are quite right. However, as yet, I have no children."

"No daughters, either?"

Griffydd hid his surprise at the man's choice of words. "No children at all."

"A careful sort you are, then, and wise, too."

Griffydd thought of the drain on Dylan's purse his children caused, and nodded.

"Seona will have fine dowry, although not as much as she's worth. And of course, she's a virgin."

Griffydd busied himself cutting the meat and said nothing, reminding himself that he had not wanted to speak of love and marriage.

Obviously his mind was not particularly astute tonight. He should have talked of other matters, like shipbuilding and the Lowlanders' new design, rather than marriage.

Still he supposed it was inevitable that Diarmad would mention Seona sooner or later, if he wanted a marriage alliance. Griffydd would have preferred later, and he couldn't help wondering if he had betrayed too much when he had first laid eyes on her.

"But enough of this talking!" Diarmad cried, garnering the attention of all in the hall as he rose and lifted his drinking horn. "To an alliance between the Gall-Gaidheal of Dunloch and the Welsh of Craig Fawr!"

The rest of the men got to their feet, including Griffydd, and drank.

Diarmad threw himself back into his chair, while Griffydd remained standing and addressed his host. "If you will excuse me, Diarmad, I believe I should retire. It has been a long journey, and tomorrow we have much to discuss."

Diarmad nodded. "As you wish." He snapped his fingers and called, "Seona! Show our guest to his quarters!"

Despite his amazement that Diarmad would call his own daughter in such a contemptuous fashion, Griffydd tried to keep any surprise from his face. He was also shocked that she would be given the task of escorting a male visitor to his sleeping quarters.

For her part, Seona did not move. She regarded her father with a blank expression, as if she had not really heard his command. Nevertheless, Griffydd thought he saw a gleam in her eye that indicated otherwise.

He pondered his next move, whether to ask for another escort, or have her light his way. Quickly and surreptitiously he scanned the hall.

Everyone had stopped eating and drinking to look at him, some with obvious scorn, some with undisguised curiosity. Interestingly, none of their attention was on Seona.

This was another test, he thought.

"I am pleased you recognize that I am a man of honor who can be trusted to treat your daughter with the respect she deserves,'' he said to Diarmad, bowing slightly.

Then he turned his unruffled gaze onto Seona, thinking the next decision was hers.

Seona said nothing. She merely took hold of a nearby rush torch and stuck it into fire, lighting it before going to the door to wait for him.

Griffydd bowed to his host and followed her outside.

Chapter Three

Reluctantly Seona led the way to the longhouse where Diarmad MacMurdoch's guests were customarily housed. It was outside the walls of the fortress, beside the pine wood that bordered a stream that flowed down from the hills toward the sea.

Holding the flickering torch, she tried to concentrate on the rough ground, and not to be so conscious of Griffydd DeLanyea's proximity as they walked together in the pool of light. Nevertheless, she felt as if they were the only two people for miles around.

The rhythmic pounding of the waves upon the nearby shore filled her ears and would have been soothing at any other time. Now it seemed the echo of her own throbbing heartbeat.

Then she realized there was another sound. Griffydd DeLanyea, wrapped in his dark cloak like a spirit of the night, awesome and compelling and frightening all at once, was singing an *iorram,* a rowing song of her father's men. The low, soft pulses of the cadences were familiar and yet different sung in his fine deep timbre. There was a melancholy to his voice, an inward sadness that seemed to tug at an answering loneliness deep within her.

But how could he, obviously a rich and respected son of a nobleman, understand the loneliness that was her daily lot?

Then he stopped singing and the sudden quiet moved her to speak. "You sing well."

His steps hesitated a moment, as if he had not been aware of what he was doing. "Thank you."

"I have heard that all the Welsh are fine singers."

"Many are," he concurred bluntly.

There seemed little willingness on his part to continue the conversation. She had no wish to force him to speak if he would rather not, so they continued in silence until they reached the longhouse.

She pulled back the heavy woolen covering and slipped inside. As he followed, she put the rushlight in a sconce in the wall, illuminating the furnishings of the longhouse: the trestle table, the benches and stools, the beds against the wall and Griffydd De-Lanyea's baggage in the corner.

She turned and faced her father's honored guest.

She was not tall enough to see eye-to-eye with him; instead, the first thing to meet her gaze was his full, sensual lips, which were not smiling. She forced herself to look at his dully shining chain mail, the gray metallic glitter reminiscent of its owner's eyes.

"This seems rather a large edifice for one man to inhabit, even temporarily," he observed.

"Yes, well," she stammered, "most of my father's guests bring some men with them."

"An entourage?"

She flicked a glance at his enigmatic face. "Yes."

He wrapped his arms about his body in a way that seemed almost...protective.

Could he be feeling as she did? Could he sense the current of tension that ran between them, the strange excitement?

That notion sent a thrill through her, and she found it easier to draw breath and to look at his face.

"I am very tired. If you will excuse me, my lady," he said, bowing his head.

She was curiously reluctant to make a hasty retreat, so she decided to correct his mistake.

"You are wrong, sir," she said softly.

"What's that?" he asked, clearly taken aback.

"I am not a lady."

"You are Diarmad MacMurdoch's daughter, are you not?" he queried, strolling away as if to familiarize himself with his new quarters.

With his attention elsewhere, she relaxed a little more.

"Oh, yes," she replied, a hint of bitterness creeping into her voice. "Although he would rather I was not. However, he is not a lord, so I am not a lady. Still, I thank you for the compliment."

When he did not respond, she said, "I would have

expected a man of your rank to have quite a large party with him.''

"I hope you are not implying I would need their protection? Or do you fear I might be lonely?''

"Oh, no,'' she hastened to assure him. "You are too valuable to be at risk, at least physically.'' She paused as he examined an unlit oil lamp hanging from a beam. "And I think you are used to being alone.''

He chuckled so softly she could barely hear him.

"Indeed, I often find my own company the most satisfactory,'' he replied, glancing at her briefly. "How is it you could perceive that, I wonder?''

"Because you came here alone,'' she replied.

"And perhaps because we share that trait?'' he proposed, turning to regard her, his expression still betraying almost nothing.

"Perhaps.''

"So, Seona, do you live in a vast, empty building?''

She shook her head. "I live in a very small building.''

He raised one eyebrow quizzically. "It must make for close quarters.''

Now it was she who chuckled softly. "I live by myself in my own house at the edge of the village close to the broch.''

"Broch?"

"The ruined tower, my lord.''

"Sir,'' he said. "I am *Sir* Griffydd DeLanyea. I

will not be a lord until my father dies and I am made baron.''

"Sir Griffydd," she conceded softly, and with a nod of her head.

"Griffydd."

She stared at him a moment, befuddled.

"Griffydd," he repeated. "You may use my name, if you would like."

"Griffydd," she amended.

He shifted his weight a little and cocked his head as he continued to regard her. "If I am not at risk physically, I wonder how else I might be in jeopardy?"

She shrugged her slender shoulders, then gave him a shrewd look. "I believe from what you said in the hall, you already know." She hesitated, suddenly unsure what else she should say.

But she was determined to say *something* in her own defense.

"If my father implies that I am in any way a part of this trading pact," she averred, "he does so without my knowledge."

Griffydd's eyes widened slightly. "Without your knowledge?"

"Yes," she answered with a nod.

"You have the Sight, then?"

She gave him a puzzled look. "No."

"Are you a witch?"

"Certainly not! I am a Christian, like you."

"I am relieved to hear it, and yet confused, too."

Seona didn't know what to make of him. "I have spoken clearly enough."

"But what explanation have you?" he asked meditatively.

"Have I for what?" she demanded, her frustration with his enigmatic pronouncements growing.

"You would warn me against something of which you claim to be ignorant."

She flushed hotly. "Surely you can guess what I meant," she said. "I do not want to be a part of any offers my father might make."

"I prefer not to make assumptions, of any kind," he replied, coming closer.

In a moment, he was near enough for her to reach out and touch and she found that, despite her annoyance, her mouth had suddenly turned as dry as a salted herring.

"So, you do not approve of your father using you?"

She nodded wordlessly.

"Is this a general principle by which you live, or is it that you do not approve of me?"

"It has nothing to do with you."

He raised a quizzical eyebrow. "I wonder if I should be pleased by that response, or not?"

"I do not seek to insult you, or flatter you, either," she replied firmly. "I want you to understand that, regardless of anything my father might say, I do not consider my duties to extend beyond the honorable bounds of hospitality."

"I see," the Welshman murmured, gazing at her with the merest hint of a smile on his face. "I suppose what you are saying means that you do not intend to stay the night with me?"

"No!"

"I would have sent you away anyway," he replied solemnly. "Being a nobleman has certain responsibilities, too, especially when one is a guest. I would never assume that I would be welcomed into the bed of my host's daughter—although I must confess I have never been so tempted to forget the bounds of courtesy."

She swallowed hard, very aware that he was gazing at her face, and that she was no beauty. His words might be only empty flattery, and yet at his softly spoken compliment, heat poured through every limb.

She also knew she was smiling like a ninny, knew she must look besotted, but she couldn't help it. No man's words had ever meant so much to her—and surely the sincere approval she saw in his eyes could not be a trick.

He gently took hold of her shoulders and drew her close, bending lower. "Your scruples do you credit, Seona. Beautiful, beautiful Seona."

The moment his lips touched hers, she seemed to melt like wax in a molten flame. She could no more have turned away from his kiss than she could have willed the planets to stop their circling of the earth.

One of his hands brushed through her hair as the other stroked her back. Willingly, eagerly, she leaned toward him and returned his passionate kiss. His cloak opened and she splayed her hands on his broad chest, feeling it rise and lower beneath her outstretched palms.

With growing urgency, his mouth moved over hers and when his tongue pressed against her sealed lips, she answered his silent request, parting them to let his tongue slide into her warm and waiting mouth.

A low moan escaped her as he clasped her to him as if he would meld them together like beings made of clay.

Then, suddenly, he stopped.

Gasping, uncertain, she looked at him questioningly, her lips still tingling from his kiss.

Griffydd drew a ragged breath and pushed her away, astonished at the desire surging through him. He had never felt like this. Never! Something had to be wrong with him—or with her.

"Have you bewitched me?" he demanded. "Have you put some kind of spell upon me?"

"What…what do you mean?" she asked in a whisper.

"As tempting as the thought of sharing my bed with you may be, I am an honorable man, and I will not be seduced by my host's daughter."

"I am not seducing you!"

His hands curled into angry fists at his side and he fought to control his raging temper. Diarmad must have ordered her to escort him here as part of a dastardly scheme to force a wedding between them and therefore an alliance between his father and the Gall-Gaidheal. "Where is the jealous suitor? Or will it be your irate father who is supposed to burst in and accuse me of dishonoring you?"

She stared at him in disbelief at his accusations and the sudden change in his manner.

"For a woman who claims she does not agree with her father's strategy, you seemed very eager to give yourself to me," he continued, wrapping the cloak about himself again. "Or perhaps that kiss was only to whet my appetite?

"Unfortunately for you, his plan will not succeed. Although sleeping with you would be a serious breach of courtesy, to the Welsh making love before marriage is not enough to extort a betrothal."

"No! No—*you* kissed *me!*" she protested, dismayed by his suspicion.

"Why did you linger here at this hour of the night? And such enthusiasm to voice your honorable honesty!" he replied sarcastically. "Very clever and very crafty, Seona. Perhaps you think I am feebleminded not to see exactly what kind of trap this is? My father warned me about Diarmad MacMurdoch. It is to be regretted that he didn't give me similar warnings about *you.*"

"Because there were no warnings to be given!" she retorted, angered by his implications. "I meant what I said. I wanted you to know that I have no hand in any of my father's scheming."

"No?" Griffydd demanded, his cold, skeptical

gaze wounding her more than a dagger might have done. "Then what plan of your own were you hatching?"

"None!" she cried, glaring at him and hating him for not believing her. "This is to be the thanks I get for trying to be honest with you?"

She thought of the look in his eyes when he called her beautiful and marveled at her gullibility. "I should have realized you were not to be trusted—"

"*I* am not to be trusted? If there is duplicity here, look to yourself!"

"I am not the one spouting lies!" she replied, turning on her heel to leave.

He grabbed her arm to halt her progress and came to stand before her.

"I am an honest man, but that does not mean I am a fool. Now tell me what lies I have told," Griffydd commanded with more angry animosity than even his own parents would have suspected he possessed.

But angry he was, and hurt and upset. He had been tricked by a lovely woman, a woman he still desired so much that, despite her deceit, it was all he could do not to carry her to his bed.

He must be going mad, driven slowly insane by Diarmad MacMurdoch and his desirable daughter, who stood defiantly before him, proud as a queen, bold as an Amazon.

"Take your hands from me!" she ordered scornfully.

He obeyed at once. "What lies have I told?" he demanded again.

Her lip curled and passionate anger burned in her large eyes, although her tone was coolly sarcastic. "Since I am so tempting, *sir,* I had best leave you to your rest. Sleep well."

With that, she marched haughtily out the door.

After she had gone, Griffydd stood motionless for a long time before he raked his trembling hand through his hair.

Even now, he half expected a gang of Gall-Gaidheal led by a belligerent Diarmad to charge into his quarters and demand that he wed Seona or die.

He had been trapped like the most naive dupe in Britain.

Then he stared at his quivering fingers as if they belonged to somebody else. Indeed, he almost felt they must.

His was the steady hand. He never trembled, not with fear or longing or excitement.

Dylan did. And Dylan was the lover, never without a woman. Not him.

Yet Griffydd knew he had acted as impulsively as Dylan ever had. At the time, he had given no thought to the ramifications of kissing Seona MacMurdoch.

He had acted with his heart, not his head.

Which was wrong. And weak. And foolish. Most of all, foolish.

Her presence in his quarters had to be part of a

strategy, and her apparent sincerity only a trick.

Despite Seona's denials, she must have been a willing participant in the plan. After all, no one had shoved her through the door or asked her to stay.

Griffydd slowly drew his sword from its scabbard. With deliberate movements he twisted it to and fro until his hand grew steady again.

Until he was master of himself again.

Disgusted with his own gullibility, Griffydd told himself he would think only of the trade pact. He would ignore Seona MacMurdoch, with her fascinating face, spirited manner and huge brown eyes.

She had deceived him once, and he would not let that happen again.

Seona came to a halt on top of the rise overlooking the harbor of Dunloch near the ruined broch. The cold air blew through her loose dress and whipped her hair about her face. It howled through the gaps in the stones of the ancient tower like the keening of mourning women before heading toward the fortress and village below. In the village, a few flickering lights occasionally shone out into the darkness of the night. The sound of drunken singing rose from her father's hall, telling her that her father was in a jovial mood, obviously anticipating a considerable profit from his pact with the Welshman's family.

Wrapping her arms about herself for warmth, her gaze moved to the boundless ocean, its shimmering water lit by the pale moon.

If only she could sail away from here, or run away to some place where she could be free—of her duties, of her father, of his constant disapproval, of his plans and schemes.

But where could she go, a lone woman with no friends and no money? Her brothers would send her home, too afraid of losing command of their villages if they offended their father to shelter her. No other chieftain would want to risk his wrath, either, because Diarmad MacMurdoch commanded a large fleet. He had the ships, the men and the arms, as well as the money for more, if he chose to punish them.

Nor could she count on sanctuary in a holy place. The priests had endured many attacks over the years from the Norsemen and were all too grateful for Diarmad MacMurdoch's protection. They would certainly tell him where she was, if nothing else, and then her father would come for her. She could envision him dragging her out of a chapel, the priests helpless to stop him.

Now she had made things even worse.

She had been a fool, a simpleton so moved by her attraction to a handsome stranger that she had been totally humiliated while trying to do good.

Yet whose fault was that, really? If she were in his place, what would she make of such a visit and her willing kiss?

She should be glad he had been angry, otherwise who could say what more she might have done?

At least all that had resulted was anger on both sides, and grave suspicion on his.

She smiled sardonically. Considering her father's ability to get the best of men with whom he bargained, Griffydd DeLanyea should be thankful that she had roused his distrust. Surely now he would be twice as wary....

She gasped and her hand flew to her lips. What if he told her father what had happened in his quarters to rouse that mistrust?

Her father didn't like her as it was. Surely he would consider anything that interfered with his trade negotiations unforgivable.

This time, she might finally incur such wrath that the consequences would be more than having to listen to him berate her.

Maybe he would take away her little house. It had been very difficult to persuade him to let her live in solitude so that she did not have to endure gossip and speculation.

Perhaps he would send her to a convent. He had threatened to do so countless times; this might finally drive him to do it.

Seona shivered as she made her decision.

Somehow, she would have to insure that Griffydd DeLanyea did not tell her father what had happened in the guest quarters tonight. No matter how much more humiliating it would be to have to speak with the Welshman again, she simply could not risk the alternatives.

Chapter Four

As the light of early morning struggled through the low clouds, Griffydd groggily trudged through the spruce trees toward the stream near his quarters. Clad in breeches, plain tunic and boots, his cloak slung over his shoulder, he could hear the water babbling like the sly laughter of sprites making sport of him.

He frowned darkly. He had lain awake for a long time last night deciding how best to proceed with the negotiations, even as he had tried not to contemplate Seona. Or the kiss they had shared. Or the softness in her eyes as she had looked at him, and the way that tender, yearning expression had seemed to touch his soul.

Diarmad MacMurdoch was a despicable old villain, setting his daughter as a trap and, Griffydd knew, only a fool would continue to be a victim of her allure.

He paused a moment and drew in a breath of the piney air. The clouds looked to be moving off and the air was bracingly cool for spring. In the near distance, the stream gurgled on.

He sighed deeply and rotated his aching neck. Almost groaning aloud, he hoped a wash in the cold water would help clear his befuddled head.

He came out of the trees and immediately halted at the sight that met his eyes.

There, beside the stream a short distance away, a shaft of sunlight illuminated Diarmad's daughter as she cradled an infant in her arms.

In a plain gown as green as the trees around him, Seona regarded the babe she held with downcast eyes. Her thick, magnificent hair was drawn away from her face to fall in two twisted coils down her back, glowing in the early morning sunlight like a halo. He had never seen anything quite so breathtaking, except perhaps his first glimpse of Seona MacMurdoch's half eager, half questioning eyes.

She looked like a Madonna with child, and the sight brought such a longing to Griffydd that it seemed a lump the size of the Stone of Scone had suddenly lodged in his throat.

It took him another moment to realize she and the baby were not alone. Another young woman squatted a short distance away, washing a garment in the fast-moving and no doubt chilly stream. She was, he saw at once, what other men would call beautiful, with a fine profile and long slender neck emphasized by her dark hair braided about her head. As she worked briskly, it was evident her body was shapely, too.

A little boy played beside her with a stick in the water, and the woman paused to admonish him, a petulant frown on her face. Beautiful, perhaps, but it was the patient smile on Seona's visage as she called the lad to her side that appealed to him more.

Suddenly the toddler slipped on the rocky bank and fell into the stream. The other woman emitted a shriek as the swift current caught his body, carrying him away from her.

Seona, still holding the infant, scrambled to her feet while Griffydd threw off his cloak and charged into the rushing water. When the little boy's head disappeared beneath the surface, the other woman screamed hysterically.

Concentrating on the child, Griffydd judged where the current would send its victim and hurried there, scanning the cold, rushing water as he had been taught to do when catching fish if he were forced to fend for himself.

There!

The child's head popped up, and at once Griffydd reached down and scooped the boy out of the frigid stream. The boy choked and sputtered as he clung to Griffydd.

"I've got you. You're safe," Griffydd muttered in Welsh, too shocked himself by the sudden and unexpected need to rush to the rescue to remember that the little fellow wouldn't understand a word he said. He walked carefully toward the bank, lest there be more loose stones underfoot.

The boy stared up at Griffydd with wide, terrified eyes, his lips blue as his breathing returned to normal. Griffydd rubbed the child's arms with his free hand, trying to warm him as best he could.

The other young woman pushed past Seona and ran to them, grabbing the boy from Griffydd's grasp as a jumble of grateful Gaelic tumbled from her lips.

Trying not to remember the last time he had spoken to Seona, Griffydd gathered up his cloak as she hurried closer.

He coughed and discovered he had no stone in his throat, after all. "Tell her to wrap the child in this."

Smiling with obvious relief, Seona nodded and spoke to the woman, who took the cloak and did as he ordered.

"Thank you!" Seona said fervently, turning back to him as she gently rocked the whimpering infant in her arms.

"It was nothing."

The boy stopped shivering and stuck a finger in his quivering mouth before regarding his savior pensively, one damp arm tight about the woman's neck.

"Fionn and his mother don't think so," Seona observed, nodding at them. She spoke a few rapid words of Gaelic, and Griffydd recognized his name. Obviously, introductions were being made.

"These are both her children?" Griffydd inquired.

"Yes. She is Lisid, and they are hers."

Lisid continued to smile at him, brushing a stray lock of dark hair from her pretty face with a gesture that was surprisingly coy, given that her child had almost drowned only moments ago.

"This is Fionn," Seona said, nodding at the boy. She smiled down at the infant she held. "And this little angel is his sister, Beitiris."

Seona glanced up at Griffydd, then away, as a lovely blush crept over her smooth cheeks, like the pink that tinted the clouds he used to watch out the window of his bedchamber when he would waken with the dawn.

He did not know what to make of her bashful demeanor here beside the stream. Changeling, indeed, to be so seemingly modest one moment, a spirited maiden the next and a brazen temptress after that, he thought with a twinge of bitterness.

"I will leave you to your ablutions," he said abruptly, turning to go.

"No, please, wait a moment!" Seona cried when he had gone a few paces.

He stopped and glanced over his shoulder. He was not the only one taken aback by her sudden outcry, for Lisid's expression was one of surprise, too.

"I...I wish to speak with you, Sir Griffydd," Seona stammered. Then she ran her gaze over him and frowned. "Unless you are too cold and wet. Perhaps later..."

His lips twitched in what Seona thought was supposed to be a smile. "I have been trained to endure the cold, and a Welshman doesn't mind the wet. If you have something you wish to say to me, I would rather hear it now—when I have a witness.''

Blushing at his implication, Seona asked Lisid to excuse her. With a somewhat reluctant look, Lisid set Fionn down on the ground, then took Beitiris, leaving Seona free to follow after Griffydd.

As he waited for her, his visage impassive, standing as motionless as one of the rocks of the hills around her, clad only in an unlaced, short-sleeved tunic belted over breeches yet apparently oblivious to the chill of the morning, Seona hugged herself for warmth, and comfort, too. This was not going to be easy, despite his rescue of Fionn.

''What is it?'' he asked when she reached him, as if she were a servant offering something for which he had no need.

She swiftly checked to see that Lisid was in sight yet out of hearing. ''I have to speak to you of what happened last night.''

Still his expression did not alter. ''What of it?''

''Were you intending to tell my father?''

Griffydd raised one eyebrow quizzically.

''Please don't.''

She saw a flash of emotion in his gray eyes, but what it was exactly, she could not be sure.

''Then you continue to assert that you stayed of your own accord?'' he asked evenly. ''Perhaps I should compliment you on your boldness—but I would rather not.'' He looked past her to Lisid.

"What a pity she is there. If she were not, you could attempt to seduce me again."

Flushing even more—although whether with shame or at the notion of being in his arms again, she didn't want to consider—Seona forced herself not to say anything in hasty anger. "Please, Sir Griffydd—"

"Griffydd. After that kiss, I think we have no need of titles."

Although his words made her burn with shame, she wished he would shout at her or at least appear angry instead of just standing there as calmly as if they were discussing the price of wool.

She drew herself up, deciding she would not demean herself further by seeming to beg. "I would appreciate it if you did not speak of last night to my father. Otherwise, I will rue it greatly."

Griffydd DeLanyea's eyes narrowed ever so slightly.

"It was by his order that you escorted me to my quarters," he reminded her.

"It was most certainly not by his order that I voiced my unwillingness to be used."

"Are you telling me that he will punish you for that?" he charged, his voice low, yet firm and commanding. The voice of a lord. A king.

"For trying to warn you, of course."

"How?"

"Does it matter?"

He eyed her speculatively. "No doubt if I reveal my own lack of proper behavior, he will be mollified.

Indeed, he should be quite pleased to know his plan was so effective.''

''No!'' she cried sharply, angry tears welling in her eyes.

Again his expression altered ever so slightly and she thought she saw a glimmer of genuine concern on his handsome face. ''I would not allow him to hurt you.''

She gazed at him with undisguised surprise. ''*You* would not allow him?''

''No, I would not,'' he said with such conviction she could believe that a stranger she barely knew would protect her from her father's wrath.

Before she could respond, they heard a commotion in the trees near them along the path leading from the fortress to the stream.

''DeLanyea!''

Her father came charging out of the pine trees like a hunted boar, his men trailing behind him, and a grin split his broad face as his shrewd gaze darted between an apparently impassive Griffydd DeLanyea and a flushed Seona.

''Well met!'' he shouted happily, addressing the Welshman.

''When you were not in your quarters, I thought you might be here,'' he said as he came to a halt. ''And Seona, too.''

He glanced somewhat sternly at Lisid and her children, as if wondering what the devil they were doing there.

Naoghas, Lisid's husband, seemed far from pleased to note their presence, too.

Even at this distance, Seona could see Lisid's petulant frown as she tossed her lovely head before hurrying away, leading a reluctant Fionn by the hand.

"I was helping Lisid with her children," Seona explained, "and Sir Griffydd came to wash.

"It was a good thing," she went on, looking at Naoghas as much as her father, "for Fionn fell in the stream and might have drowned if Sir Griffydd had not rescued him."

"Is this so?" Diarmad cried. "Then it is well you were here. You have my thanks, DeLanyea."

"And mine," Naoghas said, albeit with less than good grace. "I am Lisid's husband," he added with a slightly belligerent tone, for Naoghas was a fiercely jealous man.

Seona wondered what Sir Griffydd made of him. Unfortunately, she could get no clue at all to that, or anything else the man might be thinking as he bowed his head in greeting.

"Our guest still has not yet had a chance to perform his ablutions," Seona said, anxious to get away from her slyly grinning father and his men, as well as the confusing, infuriating, compelling Griffydd DeLanyea.

"Oh?" Diarmad responded, as if it were inconceivable that a man would want to wash.

"Perhaps we should leave him to do so in peace."

"I would appreciate that," the Welshman said evenly.

"I was thinking we should hunt this morning, while the weather is so fine," her father remarked. "Plenty of time to talk of trade later."

"If you wish," DeLanyea replied.

"Good, good!"

"Unfortunately, I had not thought to bring my hunting weapons."

"We will give you spears and one of our finest horses," Diarmad offered.

Griffydd DeLanyea laid a hand on his breast and bowed. "I am honored by your generosity."

Diarmad cleared his throat loudly. "I, um, am pleased to let you have the loan of them."

Seona started to walk away, vaguely attempting to think of ways to occupy her time while the men were hunting. She hoped Griffydd DeLanyea would say nothing to her father about last night. She prayed she could trust him to keep silent.

Thankfully, the fleeting expression of concern she had seen on his face before her father had arrived made her think her hopes were not unfounded.

In the meantime, she could help Lisid with the dying of cloth, or Maeve with baking bread, or assist in the drying of the day's catch—

"Seona!" her father barked.

She halted abruptly and turned to face her suddenly irate parent. "I have not given you permission to go."

Blushing again, she wondered what he was doing, beyond humiliating her by treating her like a child.

"If you will excuse me, Father, Sir Griffydd," she said, trying to be as inscrutable as the Welshman as she dipped her head in a bow, "I have many things to do."

"Go to my hall and wait for me," her father ordered, waving her away as if she were one of his dogs.

Or perhaps not even as important as that.

Griffydd didn't watch Seona leave. Instead, he kept his attention on his host and Lisid's husband.

He had to keep his wits about him. He had to remember that he was here to conclude a trade agreement between his father and MacMurdoch, not to interfere in the man's family.

It should not matter a whit to him how Diarmad treated Seona. He should not have implied he would come between her and her father, even if the man did speak to her as if she were his servant, or a slave.

Perhaps this was all part of the plan. Maybe they were trying to make him feel sympathy for her. Despite her protestations, it might even be that the only reason she had spoken to him this morning was because she had failed in her objective to seduce him in order to force a marriage, and she didn't want her father to know that.

Clearly, he dare not let down his guard against her, despite the proud, pleading look on her face when she asked him to keep silent, or the equally proud resentment that flashed in her eyes when her father sent her away so rudely.

"Well, a fine day for stag hunting it is, and no mistake," Diarmad declared. "I'll leave you now to wash, and we shall meet in my hall to break the fast."

Griffydd bowed in acknowledgment while Diarmad strode away, followed by his silent warriors, including Naoghas, who gave Griffydd a hostile glance before he disappeared through the trees.

Although Griffydd had saved the man's son, he was a foreigner, a Welshman with Norman blood in this land of Gall-Gaidheal and Scot. That could be cause for animosity.

No warrior of any discernment would doubt that Griffydd DeLanyea was well-trained and a good fighter, so jealousy was always a possibility.

Or perhaps it was another type of jealousy that raised Naoghas's animosity.

The vision of Seona in a passionate embrace with the dark-haired, stocky, morose Naoghas sent a cascade of emotions pouring through Griffydd, none of them good. Jealousy, anger, hatred—things he had not felt so strongly in his life.

Then he remembered the beauteous Lisid, and her grateful smiles.

He rubbed his forehead with frustrated dismay. Of course, the man was jealous of his wife—yet he had thought of Seona first. He *must* be going mad!

Griffydd turned on his heel and in one long stride

reached the stream. He yanked off his tunic and threw it to the ground, then knelt on the bank and splashed his face with the frigid water.

It did nothing to cool the fires burning within him.

He sat back on his haunches and stared unseeing across the stream at the rocky hill on the other side, willing himself to regain his self-control. To put Seona MacMurdoch out of his mind.

It was a good thing Dylan wasn't here, he reflected sourly. His foster brother always claimed Griffydd had a stone where his heart ought to be, and surely the only reason women went with him was because they surmised he was rock hard elsewhere, too.

Griffydd, of course, never rose to the bait of Dylan's teasing, nor did he reveal how much his foster brother's words disturbed him. He had a heart, he knew—did he not love his parents, who were the finest people in England? Did he not love his home, his country, his siblings—aye, and Dylan, too? It was just not his way to proclaim his feelings to any and all who would listen.

Nor did he get his women pregnant.

Dylan thought that odd, until one of Griffydd's lovers confided that Griffydd always withdrew. He found it incredulous that Griffydd would rob himself of that great delight. After all, what did it matter if the woman got with child? No shame to a Welshwoman or the child, and none to him, if he did his duty and provided for them.

Dylan would never understand. Love was not a

game or sport to Griffydd. A woman's heart was not some kind of toy, and a child simply another possession. A woman's love and the birth of a child brought with them duty and responsibility, as well as happiness.

Griffydd shook his damp hair like a dog, as if he could rid his mind of his troubles like droplets of water.

Vowing to keep his mind only on matters of business, and not on confusing, disturbing women, or their families and their friends, Griffydd drew on his tunic and marched grimly back to his quarters.

Chapter Five

Aghast, Seona stared at her father incredulously as she faced him in the empty hall.

"Don't look at me like I asked you to cut off a finger," her father growled.

"I will not take them!" she muttered through clenched teeth, glancing at the pile of clothing on the table beside him. "I did what you asked of me last night, but I will not go to Griffydd DeLanyea's quarters again! It would not be seemly."

"You will if I order you to!" her father commanded.

She took a deep breath and tried to restore some measure of calm. It was no good shouting at her father. He simply shouted back, and louder. The last thing she wanted was for anybody outside to hear what her father was proposing.

"Girl, you will do as I say!" Diarmad ordered angrily, bringing his fist down on the table so hard it rattled. "They are my gifts and you have to show him how to don them properly."

"Surely a man of his age can dress himself without my help," she retorted.

"Not the *brat!* What if he does it wrong and it falls off? We don't want him shamed!"

"Oh, no, we cannot be having that!" she replied, her face flushed with righteous indignation. "Shame me by treating me as goods to be bartered, shove me at him like a breed sow, but don't let *him* make a mistake with his clothes!"

Her father suddenly reached out and grabbed her arm roughly. "Listen to me, Seona!" he hissed. "You'll do as I say, or by God, you'll regret it!"

"What will you do?" she cried passionately, trying to wrest her arm from his tight grasp. "Hit me?"

Her father's brows lowered ominously, but she was too upset to care.

"Is that what you did to my mother before she ran away?"

"She ran off with another man, as you well know," he growled. "She left you here with me, so you had better do what I say, or I'll have you put in a convent to rot."

"Maybe I would prefer to rot there than exist here!"

"Very well! That can be arranged—but until then, you will do as I command, and I want you to help that grim-faced Welshman don the *brat.*" With his free hand, Diarmad gathered up the clothing. "Come!"

He marched toward the door, pulling her with him.

"Wait!" she protested. "I'll do what you ask, but don't drag me through the village like a dog."

He halted and gave her a narrow-eyed glare as he let go and handed her the clothing. "It is time you saw sense."

As she went to the door, his next words sounded like a curse.

"At least we know he's not going to make improper advances. He cannot even bring himself to look at you."

Griffydd briskly rubbed his legs with a piece of rough linen, warming them. God's wounds, that water had been cold!

Since his unforeseen dash into the stream, a cool wind had arisen, blowing in across the harbor. As a result, this vast longhouse was scarcely much warmer than outside, especially when one was naked.

It had seemed to take forever to get a fire lit in the hearth, and his shivering had not helped.

He thought of all the times Sir Urien Fitzroy, said to be the finest trainer of fighting men in England and an old friend of his father's, had insisted they continue their arms practice in the chilling rain or even snow. When Dylan had grumbled that Fitzroy was trying to kill them slowly, he had reminded them that battles were not always fought in fine weather, and that sometimes a man had to fend for himself if he got separated from his army, which meant traveling cold and wet and hungry.

While Griffydd could appreciate the reasoning, he had hated every minute of Fitzroy's lessons of endurance.

As Griffydd reached for his breeches, he reflected that today he had done something better than fend for himself after losing his companions: he had saved a child's life.

He hoped the little boy—Fionn?—would not catch a chill, or worse.

"Sir Griffydd!"

He paused at the sound of the familiar voice. "What is it?" he called back, quickly tugging on his breeches, then his tunic and boots, as he wondered what in the name of the saints Seona MacMurdoch was doing outside his quarters, shouting his name as if it were a call to arms.

"I bring you gifts from my father!"

A sardonic smile crossed Griffydd's face before he assumed an expression of disinterest.

He pulled back the covering over the door, to see Seona standing outside with a bundle of cloth in her arms and a distinctly disgruntled look on her face.

"Gifts?" he inquired, not moving from the threshold.

She nodded briskly and held out the bundle. "Clothes," she announced. "A *leine chroich, brat* and *cuarans.*"

Obviously she did not want to be here any more than he particularly wanted to see her.

Just as it had become obvious, from the manner in which her father had spoken to her, that her relationship with her parent was a troubled one, at best. He could even believe she detested him. In fact, her father had been so harsh, Griffydd was beginning to conceive it possible that Seona meant what she said about not wanting to be a part of any plan of Diarmad's. He would not be eager to obey such a man, either.

Still she was MacMurdoch's daughter, and a Gall-Gaidheal, so he had best be on his guard. She was awaiting him alone, and that was suspicious, too.

"Thank you," he said, stepping forward.

A cold breeze caught hold of the end of the fabric in her arms, making it flap like a pennant in the wind, reminding him that he had no warm cloak to wear on the hunt because he had given it to the boy's mother. Perhaps the *brat,* which he knew was nothing more than a large piece of woven fabric, could be used instead.

He reached out to take the gifts.

She didn't give them to him. "I am to show you how to wear them," she muttered through clenched teeth.

"I know how to dress myself."

"I know you do," she retorted, not meeting his gaze. "My father ordered me to show you. He's afraid that if you don't do it properly, the *brat* will come undone and you will be shamed."

"Shamed?" he inquired lightly.

She gave him a brief, sidelong glance. "Yes. Because men do not wear anything underneath."

"You mean he fears if I attempt to put the *brat* on by myself, it will fall off?"

"Yes," she snapped, coloring.

Griffydd felt the most odd compulsion to laugh. He might have, except that Seona the Confusing was standing in front of him.

"I have to say that the notion of finding myself half-naked in front of strangers is far from appealing, especially with this wind blowing," he remarked, keeping his tone matter-of-fact. "But tell me, do you think it would be wise for me to wear the garments? I am not used to riding so attired—or unattired, I should say—and I imagine it would not be pleasant."

He thought her lips twitched, but he couldn't be sure.

All his life he had listened to Dylan chide him for being perplexing; he was beginning to understand how frustrating it could be to converse with someone whose expression revealed almost nothing.

"No, I don't imagine it would be, either," she said, regarding him with enigmatic eyes. "You might get seriously chafed."

"On the other hand, I do not want to insult anybody by refusing a gift," he replied.

She ran a speculative gaze over him. "I suppose you could wear your breeches, too."

Suddenly and unexpectedly, she smiled, and her happy expression made her even more lovely. "Then you would not require my assistance."

For some reason, this response did not please him.

"I do not wish to insult your father by refusing his gifts," he said, suddenly determined to wear the Gall-Gaidheal garments. "Therefore, I fear I have no choice but to do as he asks."

"You fear?" she replied skeptically. "I wouldn't think a man like you would be afraid of much."

"But I do take my responsibilities as a guest and as the representative of my father very seriously."

She looked unconvinced but said nothing.

"If I do not wear these clothes properly, that would shame me. I do not care to look foolish or ignorant. Will you not take pity on me and give me your assistance?"

Her eyes narrowed slightly. "I do not think you are a man to be much pitied, either."

"While I shall take that as a compliment, I truly would hate to find my clothing slipping from me."

"I could tell you how to do it," she proposed with a touch of defiance. "That way, you could not accuse me of attempting to seduce you when I am only obeying my father's command."

"Last night you told me you were defying his orders. What makes you so obedient today?"

She regarded him with a steadfastness that was definitely unnerving. "Every warrior knows there is a time to stand and a time to retreat. Today, I have chosen to retreat."

A warrior? he thought as he looked at her eyes burning with defiance. Yes, she was. She was no weakling to be protected, no frail female to run for assistance or weep like a child.

She was as much a warrior facing down her opponent as any man he had ever encountered in a tournament.

And he was not happy to think that he was the opponent.

"Very well, you can just tell me," he conceded, fighting the urge to shiver and hoping this lesson would be brief, so that he could get back inside, out of the wind. "The shirt is no mystery, is it?"

"No," she replied, and he was happy to see some of her angry scorn disappear. "It is the *brat* that is difficult for foreigners." She eyed him critically. "You're shivering."

"No, I'm not."

"Yes, you are. You had better get inside. It would not be good if you fell ill."

"I will not fall sick from a little chill."

She gave him another cynical look, then marched past him into the longhouse.

Once inside, Seona laid the clothing on a wooden chest that was part of Griffydd DeLanyea's baggage beside the bed.

She didn't want to be alone in here with him, but

she was convinced she had no choice. His lips had been turning blue outside, and he was shivering. If their guest got sick, it would be bad for the negotiations. And if he became seriously ill, it could mean trouble for her father and, through him, everyone in the village if the Baron DeLanyea thought his son's illness was caused by neglect.

When she heard Griffydd enter, she turned around and swallowed hard at the sight of the tall warrior standing just inside the door. He wore a tunic open at the neck to reveal his muscular chest, and his powerful thighs were encased in tight-fitting breeches.

She cleared her throat. "First, the *leine chroich,*" she said, her voice too shrill. She must control this stupid anxiety, she commanded herself. Somehow.

He began to peel off his tunic. Startled by his bold move, she turned so that she could not see him.

The tunic landed on the bed, then his hand reached past her for the saffron yellow shift.

"Which is the front?" he asked evenly.

"It's the same as a tunic," she replied, still not looking at him and willing her voice to sound as calm as his. "The ties are at the front of the neck."

"Very well. Now the *brat.*" He reached around her and lifted the fabric.

There was no help for it. She had to face him.

The shirt her father had provided was a large one, the hem falling to midthigh—and the neck gaped open nearly to his navel.

As she tried not to stare, a curious expression appeared on his grave face as he held up the long length of woven cloth spread across his open hands.

"This is larger than I thought," he noted pensively. "Perhaps I can manage without my breeches, after all."

To her chagrin—it had to be chagrin that made her face burn this way!—he put down the *brat,* pulled off his boots, then, still facing her, reached under the *chroich,* obviously intending to unfasten his breeches.

She was about to turn away again when she thought she saw a mocking look in his eyes.

That look challenged her.

She would not turn away now if he stood before her as naked as a newborn babe.

"I would hate to think your father or his men might believe I suffer from some kind of maidenly modesty," he remarked.

There was no possibility that anyone on God's earth would ever confuse Griffydd DeLanyea with a maiden, Seona thought, heat racing through every limb even as she tried to remain perfectly calm.

He tugged down his breeches and stepped out of them. "I'm sorry if I am shocking you," he said without a hint of remorse.

"The sight of a pair of naked legs is hardly one to shock a Gall-Gaidheal," she replied, picking up his discarded breeches and putting them on the bed with his tunic. "We need a belt."

"There is one in my chest there." He glanced at the *brat.* "Who made this? You?"

"No."

She opened the lid of the embossed wooden chest and busied herself searching among his accoutrements for a suitable belt.

With a surge of triumph, she found one wide enough to hold all the necessary folds. She turned around—and dropped the belt, for Griffydd had tied the neck of the shirt, which lifted its hem, nearly exposing...

She scarcely knew where to look as she retrieved the fallen belt. Straightening, she tossed it onto the bed, narrowly missing his head.

He deftly twisted to avoid the flying belt. "Have I done something wrong?" he asked innocently.

"No," she answered, marching past him to pick up one end of the *brat*. "Now you stand still. Hold this end to your side while I wrap the cloth around your waist."

"As you wish."

While he kept the end of the fabric in place, she began to cover him with the *brat*.

"I am reminded of something my father once told me of," Griffydd observed while she worked, perspiration wetting her back. "The people in Egypt used to wrap their dead in linen to preserve their bodies."

Seona tried to concentrate on her task. "Preserve them? For what?"

"He told me they thought they would come to life again. He saw one once."

"An Egyptian?"

"One of the bodies. The man who healed his wounds was interested in such things. He kept it in his house."

She glanced up at him sharply. "Is that true?"

"I never lie, Seona," Griffydd replied solemnly and with apparent sincerity.

She swallowed hard. "Hold this end, too, while I fetch the belt," she commanded.

"Where did this man who keeps dead bodies live?" she asked as she picked up the belt. "Not in Wales, I trust."

"In the Holy Land."

She gave him a surprised look. "Your father was there?"

"On Crusade, with King Richard. He has many interesting tales of his travels."

She had to get close to Griffydd again to put the belt around his waist over the top of the fabric while he continued to hold it in place. Buckling the belt was the worst part and she forced herself to speak so that she wouldn't think about his body, so near and so naked beneath the layer of cloth. "You admire your father?" she asked.

"Very much. He is everything a good lord should be, and more. A noble warrior, fair lord, excellent husband and the best of fathers."

Finished buckling, she began to adjust the fabric in gathers beneath the belt with brisk, businesslike movements.

"How would you describe *your* father?" the Welshman inquired.

"Chieftain of Dunloch," she answered shortly, tugging sharply on the fabric.

"Have I offended you?"

"No!"

She worked in silence, and swiftly, so that she could leave him. Fortunately, he stood impassively as she continued to fix the fabric, although she remained very aware of his hard, flat stomach and muscular back as she moved around him.

"There," she said, straightening. "We are finished."

"You have left quite a bit," he noted, twisting to look over his shoulder at the long piece of fabric that still trailed from his waist to the bed.

"That goes over your shoulder and is held with a brooch. Do you have one?"

"I have cloak pin."

"That will do."

Standing behind him, she lifted the long end of the fabric and tossed it over his shoulder. "Now I will get the pin."

She went to the chest again.

"It should be on the right, at the top."

There was a large round brooch that would be perfect. She picked it up and regarded it.

"Is that not suitable?" he asked, stepping closer.

She glanced at his questioning face, then back at the brooch. "Not at all. I was only thinking it is rather plain, considering your family's wealth and position in the world.''

"We have not always been rich. King Richard left my father for dead in the Holy Land. When he finally got back to Wales, he had very little except his land and a ruined castle. It's been the work of his life to return our family to prosperity.''

"Oh," she said, nonplussed by his words, and by the honest sincerity in his deep, thrilling voice.

With trembling fingers and biting her lip, acutely aware of his body so close to hers, she reached up to pin the *brat* to the *leine chroich*.

When her fumbling fingers finally accomplished this task and before she could move, he put his hand over hers and held it against his shoulder. His touch was gentle, but she could no more have pulled her hand away than she could have willed herself to fly.

"I believe you," he said softly, regarding her steadily.

"I...I beg your pardon?" she whispered, looking into his grave gray eyes.

"I believe you," he repeated. "I believe that you came to my quarters last night to tell me that if your father tried to use you in his bargaining, it was without your consent. I believe that you are as honorable as I am and that you are not trying to tempt me for some nefarious scheme. I was wrong to chastise you."

"I am glad you understand that I was not trying to trick or tempt you," she replied softly.

His eyes darkened. "I believe you were not trying to tempt me for some dishonest purpose, yet you do so all the same."

"I...I tempt you?"

"As for why you kissed me," he continued, his deep voice a husky whisper, "I can only hope it was because you wanted to."

"Why did *you* kiss *me?*" she countered faintly, her mouth as parched as dried herring and her legs trembling as if she had run from the shore to the broch.

His sensual lips curved up in an incredibly enticing smile.

"Because I wanted to."

Chapter Six

Griffydd meant what he said with all his heart. Her words and her manner had convinced him of the sincerity of her denials. She was not complicit in any scheme of her father's.

Therefore, he stared in shock and dismay as doubt and anger appeared on her face.

"Then you are dishonest, as I said last night!" she charged, pulling away.

Before she could flee, he blocked the door. "I would know upon what you base that accusation," he demanded.

"You lied to me!"

"So you said before and as *I* said before, I do not lie. When do you think I have spoken falsely to you?"

She stared at the ground like a petulant child. "Let me go," she muttered.

"Not until you tell me when you think I lied. I hold my honor very dear, Seona. An accusation of deception is serious indeed, especially when unjustly made.''

''Unjustly?'' she cried, raising her passionate eyes to him. ''You told me I was beautiful!''

''You are!'' he replied, dumbfounded.

The look of harsh accusation drained from her face, to be replaced by wonderment.

''Don't you know that?'' he asked, although it was obvious she did not.

''You are the only person who has ever said that to me,'' she replied softly, and he saw the pain of that truth in her frank eyes.

''Then everyone else is blind,'' he declared, as sincere in this as anything he had ever said.

She stiffened and wrapped her arms around herself. ''Or else you think *I* am,'' she retorted. ''Maybe you think a woman as homely and unwanted as I am will be an easy prey for a man like you to seduce. That you will have a little sport here among the Gall-Gaidheal, to make the time pass quickly while you negotiate your treaty. After all, the chieftain will not mind. Indeed, he is thrusting his daughter at you!''

Before he could protest or stop her, she pushed past him and ran out of the longhouse. He followed her outside, but she was gone and he couldn't see where she had fled.

He suddenly wondered how it would look to Diarmad and his men if he went chasing after Seona.

Like a fool, that is how he would look, he realized,

suddenly aware that he wore no boots. He must look foolish enough now.

Scowling, he went back inside and ran his hand through his hair, trying to think. To calm himself. To regain control.

How was he going to convince her of his sincerity?

Should he even try?

He had never felt as desirous for a woman in his life as he had for Seona moments ago, nor had he ever been so aroused as when Seona had moved around him, adjusting his *brat,* her slender fingers brushing his torso.

God's blood, he felt as if he must be under some kind of enchantment. What else would explain the way he was behaving, nearly stripping naked before her with the lustful boldness of…of Dylan!

Fortunately, he had come to his senses. Somewhat.

In an attempt to maintain his precarious self-control, he had tried to keep talking while inwardly reciting every Latin verb in all their forms that he could recall while she had helped him dress.

That had not been a complete success.

Yet she believed herself unattractive. How wrong she was!

And then another realization assailed him.

He did not want to be with the bold, intriguing Seona MacMurdoch for an hour, or a night, or even the duration of this visit.

He wanted to be with her for the rest of his life, as he had never wanted anything before.

He sat heavily on the bed and stared at the wall, unseeing.

Was this enchantment—or love?

What was happening to him? He barely knew her. To be sure, what he had learned pleased him—yet surely he needed to know more before he felt even remotely prepared to...what? Ask for her hand in marriage?

This was too sudden, too quick. Nobody ever...

His parents said they knew from the moment they first looked into each other's eyes that there was a bond between them and that bond had quickly blossomed into love.

He had little doubt that Seona felt attracted to him, or she would not respond to his passion as she did. She would be as cold as ice, never melting. Never allowing him to kiss her. Never answering his desire with such ardor.

She must care for him. Perhaps not with the same fierce longing...not yet.

He forced his mind to consider the possibility of marrying Seona logically. Coolly. Reasonably. He had always been able to do so with any other subject, and he could do so with this one.

If, when the time came for him to return home, he believed himself in love with Seona and she with him, making him the happiest, luckiest man in England or perhaps the whole of Europe—

If he still wanted to marry Seona when the negotiations were concluded and he had to leave her with her brute of a father, who didn't appreciate that his justly proud daughter was a jewel among women—

He shook his head and tried again. If he still wanted Seona's hand in marriage when he had to go back to Wales, what obstacles might there be to a betrothal between them?

His father wanted a trade alliance with Diarmad MacMurdoch; MacMurdoch wanted an alliance with Baron DeLanyea.

All *he* wanted was Seona, with her elusive charm and elfin face so often hidden behind that lustrous curtain of thick hair.

Again he tried to concentrate.

A marriage between MacMurdoch's daughter and Baron DeLanyea's eldest son would be considered a far more serious alliance than the trading pact. His father's enemies would surely try to convince other Norman lords, and perhaps even the king, that Baron DeLanyea was up to no good with the Gall-Gaidheal and the Norse, too, no doubt.

But enemies of his family would surely cast aspersions and suspicions on any marriage Griffydd made, to anyone.

Still, this was not a simple situation. He was no shepherd boy wooing a maid. He was the son of a powerful and respected baron, she the daughter of a chieftain of the Gall-Gaidheal.

Therefore, he told himself, he must be cautious. He must keep his wits about him. He must be very sure of his feelings, and hers, before he made them known, even to Seona.

In the meantime, he had to regulate his incredible yearning for this woman he scarcely knew, lest he cause difficulties for all of them.

Somehow, he silently vowed, he would.

A short time later, now also wearing the furry *cuarans* and quite unexpectedly enjoying the unusual freedom of the *brat,* Griffydd strode toward Diarmad's fortress to join the chieftain and his warriors for the hunt.

Diarmad and his men stood near a stable inside the walls of the fortress. Beside the building was a fenced area, and inside that fence, one of the finest stallions Griffydd had ever seen. The beast was pure black and pawed at the ground as if anxious for exercise.

Griffydd had to pass the entrance to the hall to get to the stable, and as he did, a woman came outside. Recognizing Lisid, and mindful of her husband's reaction that morning, as well as the fact that Naoghas was standing beside Diarmad at that very moment, he intended only to nod his head at her in greeting.

Instead, she blocked his path, just as he had stood in front of Seona not long ago.

Yet how different was this woman's sly smile, and how discomforting the measuring look she gave him.

"You look well in the *brat,*" she said, surprising him, for he thought she spoke only Gaelic.

"Thank you," he answered politely. "Forgive me, but Diarmad and his men are—"

"I made it, you know. The *brat,* that is my handiwork."

"It is very fine."

Her smile grew. "And I dyed the shirt. I am the best at such work in the village."

"Are you, indeed?" he remarked, determined to get away from her before Naoghas thought he *wanted* to stand and speak with his wife. "Now if you will excuse me, the others are waiting."

He didn't tarry to hear her response, but hurried toward Diarmad, acutely aware that Naoghas was giving him a malevolent look.

Deciding the best thing to do would be to ignore the man, Griffydd kept his attention on Diarmad, who grinned broadly.

"The *brat* looks well on you, my friend!" the chieftain declared as Griffydd joined him.

"Thank you. I fear it takes some getting used to."

"Perhaps," Diarmad answered with a chuckle. "Those of us born to it wouldn't know. Now, come, man, and pick a mount for the hunt. This weather is too fine to linger here."

"I will take that one, if I may," Griffydd answered, nodding at the black stallion.

Diarmad's eyes widened a little as if in surprise; then he seemed to stifle a smile. "Oh, I would choose another," he suggested.

Griffydd didn't like the implication of that look.

"Why? Is there something the matter with that horse?"

"Not at all," Diarmad answered, and he gave his companions a secretive glance that also riled Griffydd.

Did they believe he could not handle the horse? Or that he was afraid of so obviously spirited an animal? He had been trained to ride by his father and Urien Fitzroy, the two best teachers in England. There was no horse he could not master.

"I will take the black one, then, unless you forbid it," he challenged.

"Oh, I would not forbid a guest from picking whatever horse he would," Diarmad replied, still with that infuriating almost-grin on his broad face. "Very well, take the black. But I warn you, he has a tough mouth."

Griffydd DeLanyea's only answer was a little smirk of his own.

Sometime later, outside the longhouse of Lisid and Naoghas, which was between the fortress and the wharf, Seona stood and shifted her weight from side to side, singing softly as she tried to quiet Beitiris.

As the morning had promised, the day was sunny. There was a chilly breeze blowing, yet if one stayed out of it and in the sun, it felt like summer.

From where she stood, Seona could see the harbor and the ships rocking at the wharf. A few of the fisherman had already returned with their day's catch, and snatches of their voices traveled from the beaches, where their wives and children helped them bring the fish ashore.

Lisid had recently fed Beitiris, then handed her to Seona to burp and rock to sleep while she tended to the dying of the cloth for the *leine chroich*. It was also Seona's job to keep an eye on little Fionn, who was playing with floating twigs in one of the buckets of water Seona had filled.

Lisid needed someone to watch her children, for her work was a serious business, made more intense by the lack of saffron. It was too costly for most of the warriors to afford, so Lisid had to make do with birch leaves, or bog myrtle. The results were satisfactory, if one was skilled and careful enough.

While Lisid concentrated on the dye, Seona's thoughts were far away, with a certain member of the hunting party.

She had seen the warriors depart from a distance, not wanting to get any closer. Not daring to, because she was finding it more and more difficult to think when she was anywhere near Griffydd DeLanyea.

Yet think she must, because she had to come to some sort of conclusion regarding him and his avowed opinion of her.

Did he mean what he said about her appearance, or had her reproach been justified? As incredible as it seemed, did he find her beautiful—or did he think her easy prey for his seduction?

Humming softly, she maneuvered her way toward

one of the pots of water she had filled, but not for any reason to do with the dying of fabric. Instead, she gazed at her reflection in the still water.

She was not beautiful, not like Lisid, she mused as she regarded her own grave face. Yet she didn't believe she was ugly, either, even if she was too thin, her chin a little pointed and her eyes too large.

Her father thought her stupid, too, because she lacked the patience for weaving and had never been able to manage dying so that her cloth was evenly colored. After many hours of patient instruction from old Meigan, Seona had been pronounced hopeless and told the best thing she could do was help Lisid by keeping the pots filled, tending to the fire and taking care of the children.

Seona would far rather see to the children than watch over a pot of yellow dye.

"What are you singing? It is an *iorram?*" Lisid asked as she carefully lifted the fabric from the pot of dye boiling over the fire to check its progress.

"Yes, it is," Seona replied, turning her head to look at Fionn, and so that Lisid wouldn't see her blush.

She shouldn't be blushing, really. What did it matter what song filled her head? Lisid could not know she was softly murmuring the song she had heard Griffydd DeLanyea sing last night.

"How much longer will it be?" Seona asked.

"Not long now. Are you getting tired of holding the baby?"

"Not at all. I was only thinking of the evening meal." She glanced up at the sun. "I suppose the men will be back from the hunt before dark."

"I should think so," Lisid replied with a pert little frown as she sprinkled a bit more of the myrtle into the pot. "DeLanyea will not want to be riding long."

"He is not used to the *brat*," Seona agreed. "He might need a salve."

Lisid made a sly smile that Seona knew well.

She had never liked the vain young woman who delighted in men's attention, whether appropriate or not.

"I think that will be the least of his troubles," Lisid continued. "Did you not see the horse he rode?"

Puzzled, Seona shook her head. "Not well."

"Your father let him take his prized fighting stallion."

"That cannot be!" Seona gasped, her sudden jerk of surprise making Beitiris start to fuss.

"Well, it is," Lisid retorted smugly. "I saw him myself."

Seona began to rock from side to side to calm the infant as she tried to calm herself, too.

The fighting stallions were virtually wild, and trained to bite and kick. True, her father had them also broken to the saddle in case of extreme need, but they were never really meant to be ridden.

"He took the black stallion?" she repeated incredulously.

"So I said," Lisid replied. "I was there at the stables. I...I had to tell Naoghas something before they rode out.''

Seona doubted that, and by Lisid's hesitation, she knew that was not truly the reason she had been at the stables.

Griffydd DeLanyea was a handsome man. Lisid probably went there expecting him to notice her, the way a fisherman waits for a fish to take the bait.

By her peevish manner, Lisid must have been disappointed.

That need only mean Griffydd DeLanyea had not been blind to Naoghas's jealous displeasure when he saw them by the stream this morning. It did not necessarily prove that Griffydd had been speaking the truth when he said he found *her* beautiful.

''I really believe that Welshman is a fool,'' Lisid continued.

Lisid would undoubtedly consider that opinion vindicated if she had any inkling of what Griffydd had said to her that day, Seona thought.

''He should have seen that was no ordinary horse,'' she added.

''Didn't my father try to stop him?''

''He suggested DeLanyea take another mount.''

Seona could imagine how it was, her father getting that smirk she knew too well on his face when he suggested DeLanyea take another horse. Any man of pride would think the offer a slap at his prowess as a rider, and she was quite certain Griffydd DeLanyea possessed a considerable measure of pride, and not without justification.

Nevertheless, she wondered what had possessed her father to let DeLanyea take that fierce beast for the hunt, unless he had been hoping that the Welsh-man would break his neck. Even if Griffydd managed to stay on the horse's back, it would be difficult to control and, she would think, a most uncomfortable mount.

"That's a man with Norman blood for you, I dare-say," Lisid said coldly, glancing at Seona. "Ignorant and arrogant. And you know what else they say about Normans, don't you?"

"No," Seona answered absently, wondering how long Griffydd would manage to subdue the black stal-lion.

"It is said they prefer men."

"For what?"

Lisid gave her a significant look. "Can you not guess? It is obvious DeLanyea is not like normal men."

Seona kept her disgust from her face, both for the subject and Lisid's opinion.

Then she realized that in one way, Lisid was quite right, provided one considered the men of Dunloch the measure for what was normal. Griffydd DeLanyea was most certainly not like them.

"Even if that were so," Seona replied, "I have never heard such an aspersion cast at the Welsh. In-deed, I thought the opposite was true."

Lisid didn't answer; she only tossed her pretty head and went back to her work.

For all her concern about Griffydd's fate on the fighting stallion, Seona couldn't resist a secretive smile at Lisid's peeved reaction.

"Look!" Fionn cried suddenly, commanding their notice. He pointed at his twigs floating in rows in the bucket of water. "Look. Ships!"

Seona smiled warmly. "Lovely, Fionn. Are they fishing boats?"

He frowned as if she had just insulted him mightily. "No!"

"Ah, then you are a merchant?"

His scowl grew even darker. "No!"

"Then you are a great king and these are your longships sailing out to sea?"

His frown changed to a broad smile, and he nodded. "Like that one!" he cried, pointing in the direction of the harbor.

Seona followed his gesture, then stared, holding Beitiris close to her chest.

An unfamiliar longship had appeared around the headland.

It was one of the finest vessels Seona had ever seen, riding low in the water, its curved prow slicing cleanly through the calm harbor. Over the side of the vessel hung the round shields of Norsemen, and sunlight glinted off their metal embossings. The sound of their rowing song came clearly over the water, as did the splash of the sixteen pairs of oars, indicating a well-trained and well-commanded crew.

The ship moved swiftly closer, so swiftly Seona realized the ship would be at the wharf in too short a time to send someone for her father.

She stifled her fear. There was no reason to believe this was an enemy bent on attacking the village. It was only a single vessel entering the harbor in the daylight. And the Gall-Gaidheal were subjects of the Norse king. This ship could simply be putting in at Dunloch for supplies.

Or it could be time for Haakon to collect the scatt, the sum he demanded from her father as tribute.

Some of the tension ebbed from her body, until another dread assailed her.

Perhaps Haakon had heard of her father's intended trading alliance with a Welsh-Norman baron. Maybe he had sent this ship as a reminder of the possible retaliation against a village whose chieftain conspired against his lawful ruler.

Seona turned to Lisid, who was likewise watching the unknown ship.

"Who are they?" Lisid asked, an edge of panic in her voice. "Do you recognize the ship?"

"No." Seona handed Beitiris to her mother. "Gather all the women and children you can, and go to the hills until you are told it is safe."

There were caves there, provisioned in case of sudden attack. All the women knew where they were and how to get to them. And how to defend them, too, if need be.

"I will gather what men are in the village," Seona finished.

Fionn's face betrayed his fear and his lips quivered. Tears filled his eyes.

Seona quickly knelt before the boy. "They are probably friends," she assured the child. "Now be a brave boy and help your mother with the smaller children, won't you, Fionn? Like a warrior?"

He nodded gravely, reminding her of another warrior she knew.

She straightened. "Do as I say, Lisid. As soon as we are sure their intention is a friendly one, I will send someone for you."

Then she was gone, running toward the village, determined to find every man she could in the short time she had left before the longship reached the wharf. Whoever stepped off that ship must not know how unprotected Dunloch was.

Because her father and his warriors were off hunting stags for sport.

Chapter Seven

He had never experienced such a poor chase, Griffydd thought morosely as he struggled yet again to
bring his horse under control. The hunting party rode
through a long, narrow valley and its confines did not
please him, either, for he was reminded of all his father's stories of sudden attack and ambush under similar circumstances.

That his stallion was a large, skittish brute, clearly
used to a strong hand, increased his apprehension.
While Griffydd had no qualms about riding the beast,
he had to devote all his attention to the horse, lest it
shy or bolt.

In hindsight, he would have done better to select a
calmer mount, but Diarmad might have thought less
of him.

He would have done better to wear his breeches,
too. He had tried to get the fabric beneath his legs as
far down as the *cuarans,* yet the constant nervous
shifting of his horse made the fabric bunch. It felt as

if the skin on the sides of his knees was being rubbed raw.

And for nothing. Since leaving Dunloch, the group of hunters had not so much as sighted a rabbit, let alone a stag.

There was an all-too-simple explanation for their lack of success.

Diarmad and his warriors made more noise than a pack of excited hounds. Indeed, the dogs seemed miraculously quiet compared to their masters. Likely every deer or animal worth hunting had long ago run far away.

Worse, not a one of Diarmad's men seemed to find this at all troubling. Instead, they seemed much more interested in emptying the contents of their wineskins down their throats.

He had known, of course, that the Gall-Gaidheal were barbarians combining the savage heritage of the belligerent, pirating Norse and the fractious, proud Scots. The Normans had been Norsemen, too, once upon a time, given land in Gaul to keep them from pillaging and plundering.

Was it any wonder the Welsh felt surrounded by Vikings, constantly fearful that they would either be driven out or totally conquered, like the Picts before them?

Yet the woman he wanted was a Gall-Gaidheal, and the daughter of one of the greediest among them. What would his father say to such a union? While Baron DeLanyea saw nothing wrong with trading with Diarmad, a marriage into his family—into this gang of wild men—would surely not delight him.

He would not be able to fault his father's reservations. He would have shared them, if Dylan or his younger brother, Trystan, had been the prospective bridegroom.

Then, suddenly, one of the hounds began to bay. Griffydd's horse whinnied and reared.

The action caught the pensive Griffydd unawares and sent him tumbling to the rocky ground.

Seona waited nervously on the wharf, watching the sleek longship came closer.

Behind her stood what men were left in the village, armed like warriors: the smiths, boatbuilders, merchants and those fishermen who had already brought in their catch. She could hear their muttering and knew they were wondering what the arrival of this vessel presaged, too.

And if they would have to fight.

Seona glanced behind her at the road leading to the wood and valley beyond, where her father and his men and their guest had gone. Hopefully they would return soon.

And she hoped Griffydd DeLanyea came back in one piece.

She had enough problems of her own right at the moment to be thinking of Griffydd DeLanyea, she reminded herself, turning her attention back to the longship.

There was a man in the stern of the vessel, not steering or doing anything except looking at the shore. He was surely a jarl, for he stood with the confident poise of a commander. Exceptionally tall and broad shouldered, he had shoulder-length blond hair and a thick beard. Around his upper arm was a wide silver band, and his scarlet tunic was girded with a silver-embossed belt. Stuck through the belt was an ax, likewise inlaid with silver. Woolen breeches and fur wrapped with thongs encased his legs, each one as massive as the stones of the broch.

The man at the rudder shouted an order and instantly the oars disappeared into the ship before being raised upright, so they looked like so many lances. Then, seemingly in one motion, they were laid along the seats of the ship as it finally drifted beside the wharf.

Thankfully, there was nothing warlike in their movements, no weapons raised and no helmets on their long-haired heads.

From behind Seona, the villagers murmured with similar relief before men hurried forward to secure the ship to the wharf.

Seona stepped forth when the jarl bounded along the center of ship and jumped to the wharf, landing nearly in front of her.

Up close, he was even more imposing, almost a giant, it seemed. His red tunic looked as if it could double as a sail. His sun-brown complexion made his pale blue eyes look like they glowed while he ran a measuring gaze over her.

For a moment, she wished she had a finer dress or some jewelry to indicate that she was a chieftain's daughter.

"In the name of Diarmad MacMurdoch, chieftain of Dunloch, I bid you welcome," she declared, glad that her voice sounded firm despite her inner trepidation, and that she had kept any hint of her displeasure at his insolent perusal from her tone.

The man put his hands on his hips and continued to survey her with barely disguised scorn.

She would *not* compare the look in this man's eyes to the way Griffydd DeLanyea had regarded her on their first meeting.

"Where is that old vulture?" the man demanded in a loud, booming voice, which would do very well for issuing orders during a gale at sea but seemed distinctly unnecessary on land.

"May I ask who wishes to know?" she replied nearly as scornfully.

He cocked his head to one side. "I am Olaf Haraldson, cousin to Haakon, King of Norway. I have been sent by your king to collect the scatt."

"Greetings, my lord," she said, bowing respectfully, believing him. If a raid had been the object of his visit, they would not be facing each other. She would already be dead. "I am Seona MacMurdoch, the daughter of the chieftain of Dunloch."

"You are his daughter?"

"Yes. Regretfully, we had no word of your impending visit, my lord," she continued, making her tone somewhat humbler, "or I assure you my father would have been here to welcome you himself."

"Where is he?"

"He had business to the north. I expect him to return at any moment. In the meantime, allow me to offer the hospitality of his hall to you and your men."

Even as she said it, she wondered where they would sleep. It would surely insult Olaf if he was denied lodgings on land. She would have to ask Griffydd DeLanyea to sleep in the hall with her father's men who were not yet married. She thought that better than asking him to share his quarters with this boisterous Norseman and his crew.

Olaf's eyes narrowed. "Out stealing sheep, is he?"

Seona bristled. "No, he is not!"

"Whatever he is about," the Norseman said with a chuckle, "it will no doubt make him some profit. Well, as long as he pays the scatt, he can do as he will in this land."

Olaf glanced over his shoulder and barked an order. He faced Seona again.

"My men will set up our camp in that meadow," he said, pointing to the open area between the fortress and the woods near the stream, much closer to the village than the guest quarters.

"We have a longhouse for guests," she said.

"I prefer to sleep in my tent when I am not at

home," Olaf replied in a way that brooked no further discussion.

"Very well," Seona answered. "Would you care to partake of some refreshment in the hall while we wait for my father?"

Olaf shook his head. "No. I will see to the making of our camp."

Then he seemed to recall his manners, for he smiled and bowed. "If you will pardon me, Diarmad's daughter."

She regally inclined her head before turning and walking away. Once she was out of sight of the wharf, she released her breath slowly, and with relief—until she spotted the group of men riding down the road in the distance, her father at the head.

They approached at a leisurely pace, which had to mean that they had not yet noticed the longship. As she hurried to intercept them, she realized she could not see Griffydd DeLanyea.

She started to run.

When she reached her father, he pulled his horse to a halt.

"What the devil brings you in so much haste?" he asked, weaving slightly in his saddle. "Are the pots empty? Have you nothing to cook for the evening meal?"

She ignored the drunken chuckles of the rest of the hunting party as she scanned the group. She saw the fighting stallion, which was being led by one of the warriors. The beast pranced nervously, its eyes rolling in its head. "Where is Sir Griffydd?"

"Whose ship is that?" Diarmad demanded, suddenly staring at the harbor and just as suddenly sober.

"It is commanded by a jarl named Olaf Haraldson. He claims to be a cousin of King Haakon come to collect the scatt."

Her father's eyes narrowed. "Tall, big man, with blond hair and a voice like thunder?"

"Yes," Seona replied, nodding.

Then, to her surprise, her father grinned. "Well, well, well, I have not seen Olaf since I visited the king. Now Haakon suddenly feels the need to pry his cousin from his side and send him on such a mission, eh?"

"This pleases you?"

"That's none of your concern. Our other guest should be."

"What has happened? Where is he?"

"Poor fellow fell off his horse and hurt his ankle. I don't think anything's broken."

Her father had enough experience of wounds, whether accidental or in battle, to be considered a good judge of such things. Nevertheless, a leg wound could be disastrous if it became infected. "Perhaps it was not wise to let him ride that beast at all."

"He wanted it and wouldn't take another."

"Let us hope, then, his wound is not serious," she replied with a small hint of the anger and dismay she was feeling.

"You had better make certain it is not. You will tend to him until he is well," her father ordered.

"That would not be—"

She hesitated when she saw the annoyance in her father's eyes. She had not been prudent to criticize him in front of his men. "Where is Sir Griffydd?" she repeated.

Her father gestured widely. "Back there with Naoghas. Come, men, let us greet Haakon's cousin and make him welcome!"

With that, he abruptly wheeled his horse and rode toward his fortress, followed by all except Lisid's husband.

Since her father seemed to find the arrival of Olaf Haraldson cause for joy, not concern, Seona turned her thoughts again to Griffydd DeLanyea. She hurried toward Naoghas and found Griffydd lying on a make-shift bed made of two saplings and some pine branches. One end was lifted and tied to Naoghas's horse. The bottom trailed upon the ground. The injured man lay motionless, his face pale and his eyes shut.

"Sir?" she said, upset to see him—anyone—in such a state.

He slowly opened his gray eyes and looked at her.

Were there other eyes in the world that could make her feel as if their possessor could see into her very soul? As if those grave, gray orbs could read her innermost thoughts and fears, hopes and dreams? As if the man looking at her knew all about her past and her present, and understood. Sympathized. Cared.

Griffydd DeLanyea blinked and she forced herself to look away from his eyes. "What happened?"

"I was thrown from my horse," he replied groggily.

She scrutinized his forehead, temples and scalp, seeking any sign of an injury there to account for his speech.

Then he yawned.

He did his best to stifle it, but she saw it nonetheless.

Her eyes narrowed. "Are you in great pain?"

He glanced at his fellow hunter and she thought his lips twitched—but not with agony.

"I fear I have broken my leg," he said mournfully, and no doubt for the benefit of his obviously annoyed hunting companion.

"Hmm. I shall have to examine him," she said to Naoghas, who looked as if he were sorry Griffydd DeLanyea wasn't dead. "Please take him to his quarters."

Naoghas nodded, and slowly turned his horse toward the guest longhouse.

As she followed them, Seona wryly reflected that their guest had certainly managed to provide himself with a more comfortable means of transport than her father's fractious stallion.

"Greetings, Olaf!" Diarmad MacMurdoch cried as he dismounted and hurried toward the Norseman who was standing in the meadow watching his crew pitch their tents.

Olaf turned to face the blustery Diarmad, noting as he did so that a large number of men were with the chieftain. His warriors, without doubt, and a fierce-looking bunch.

Haakon, Olaf's cousin, king and overlord, was surely right to send him to find out what this Gall-Gaidheal chieftain was up to, and to remind Diarmad where his loyalty should lie, for Haakon's hold on the throne was precarious at best.

Diarmad had already given his sons control of much of the coast, in a series of villages from Dunloch to the north. He had made overtures to the Scots for an alliance, too, and those pirates, Clan Ruari. Now he was welcoming Welsh-Norman noblemen allied to other powerful men of England.

For the present, however, Olaf smiled broadly and clapped a friendly hand on Diarmad's shoulder. "I bring you greetings from Haakon. I feared something was amiss when you were not here to meet my ship."

Diarmad looked at him with surprise. "But I knew nothing of your coming. It is early yet to collect the scatt.

"Indeed," he continued with a frown, "I fear I have not the full amount."

Olaf kept the skeptical smirk off his face. The day Diarmad didn't have at least twice the tribute he owed the king hidden somewhere in or near his village was the day the sun ceased its progress in the heavens. "Well, there is no hurry."

"Then you will be able to stay in Dunloch for—"

"As long as it takes to collect the scatt," Olaf finished jovially.

"Excellent!" Diarmad cried.

Olaf knew full well the man was lying, but he smiled just the same.

Seona watched as Griffydd DeLanyea, one arm about Naoghas's shoulders, hobbled toward his bed. With an exhausted sigh and keeping his weight off his supposedly injured ankle, he sat heavily.

"I thank you for your help, Naoghas," Griffydd said.

A sullen frown on his face, Naoghas merely nodded as he went to the door without even a glance at Seona as he departed.

Griffydd regarded her steadily with the usual inscrutable expression on his face. "I fear that man does not like me."

"He doesn't like anybody," Seona replied, flushing at the Welshman's attentive stare.

"That would explain his rudeness to you, even if it does not excuse it. Or is he too worried about your other visitors to say one word to you?"

"Other visitors?" she prevaricated. Surely he had been too far back to hear what she said to her father.

"I hurt my foot, not my eyes. That longship in your

harbor is the finest I have ever seen, and I think those men in the meadow were not playing a game.''

This man really was too clever.

''A cousin of Haakon has come to collect the scatt,'' she said, thinking that he would find out about Olaf Haraldson soon enough anyway.

''Ah,'' he said. ''Interesting timing, since I, too, have just arrived. Do you not think so?''

Never before had anyone asked her opinion on such matters. Never before had anyone assumed she had one.

Truly, Griffydd DeLanyea was different from anyone she had ever met.

Maybe she should go, she thought as she regarded his pale, grave face. She was sure now he was not badly injured, and leaving him alone would serve him right for feigning a more serious injury.

Yet would that not be turning tail and fleeing like a coward? Would that not be giving this foreigner the upper hand?

Seona decided she would do what she had been ordered to do: tend to him.

''Stop staring at me,'' she commanded briskly. ''Lie down so that I may examine you.''

''Very well.''

''It is the right leg, is it not?''

''It isn't hurt very badly. Just a sprain.''

''Really?'' she said, swiftly untying the thong around the *cuaran* on his right calf and pulling it off none too gently.

She had been so worried about him and the possible consequences of a serious injury, and he had such a facility for discomfiting her, that she thought he deserved to suffer a little, so she did likewise with his boot, ignoring his grunt of protest. "I am surprised a mighty warrior like you would allow yourself to be treated like an old woman."

Griffydd stifled a scowl, for in a way, she was right. His ankle did hurt, yet he could have ridden back to Dunloch. However, he had been in no mood to try to control that devil of a horse again.

Suddenly Seona let his foot drop on the end of the bed, where it banged against the wood.

"Ouch!" he cried, sitting up and grabbing his now very sore ankle. "Be careful!"

"Oh, forgive me," she murmured, completely without sincerity. "And I thought you were only feigning your injury, Sir Griffydd. Obviously I was quite wrong."

"I *did* hurt my ankle, and I saw no reason to refuse the offer of assistance."

She eyed him skeptically, in a way quite new to this cherished son of a powerful baron. "But you are not averse to some exaggeration, I take it."

He silently and, truth be told, sullenly, reclined and submitted to her as she poked and prodded his ankle and shin. He was so annoyed with her judgment of his behavior and subsequent rough treatment, he wouldn't have given her the satisfaction of making a sound if she stabbed him.

A twinkle of merriment appeared in her large, usually solemn eyes. "Not that I blame you. My father should have warned you about that horse."

"That it is apparently possessed by Satan?"

She shook her head. "No. That it is a fighting stallion."

"Fighting stallion?" Griffydd said, rising abruptly on his elbows. "He did suggest I choose another, but he never told me it was a fighting stallion."

Griffydd had seen a horse fight once. Each stallion was kept in its own pen, with an empty one between. A mare in season was brought to the center pen, and then both stallions were turned loose in the main corral to fight for her.

It had not been a pretty sight, watching two magnificent animals bent on destroying each other. Their masters and those who had bet on them shouted encouragement, their blood lust as aroused as that of the animals of whom they were supposedly masters.

"I don't suppose you thought to ask why it was so lively, or why it was kept separate from the other horses?" she asked pointedly, her hands on her slender hips as she looked at him.

"I am your father's guest," he replied with a hint of his great displeasure. "He should not have shown me the horse."

"Did he present the beast as a riding horse or did you spot it in the pen and think it was for saddle?"

Griffydd scowled. "If it was not for riding, he

should have said so. I confess I am shocked he would put me at risk.''

''Do not despair, my lord. After your fall, I am quite certain he will think twice the next time one of his guests makes a similar mistake. Now I am trying to examine you, and for that I require silence.''

''Humph!''

Griffydd lay back down, seriously displeased by Diarmad's conduct.

Yet even in his annoyance and frustration, he could not ignore the pleasant sensation of Seona's touch, or the sight of her tending to him, her long hair like a curtain shielding her face from him. He wanted very much to draw back that curtain and look at her again.

And he wanted to see her regard him once more with the concern that seemed so genuine.

For once, he wished Dylan was with him, so that he could ask his foster brother for advice on dealing with the lovely, impertinent Seona MacMurdoch.

Somehow, though, he thought Seona would confound even him.

Chapter Eight

Seona moved back from the bed.

"I believe you and my father were correct, after all. It seems to be only a sprain. I thought as much when I saw you."

"You must be very skilled to be able to tell how critically a man is hurt just by looking at him," Griffydd observed.

"When a man is supposedly in pain from a leg injury and yet he can sleep, I have to think the pain is not terribly severe."

Griffydd flushed hotly, as he had not done since he was a child, and he looked away. "I *was* thrown," he muttered.

The woolen cloth over the door moved and Lisid entered the room carrying a carafe and a goblet on a tray, and something that smelled like bread, covered with a cloth.

He was not pleased by this interruption, or by

Lisid, who sauntered across the room with the most flirtatious, sinuous movements he had ever seen.

Lisid seemed not to notice that Seona was there, nor did Seona appear to find this lack of attention the insult it was.

"The chieftain said I was to bring this here," Lisid said coyly. She set down the food and drink on the table, giving Griffydd a wide smile. "I hope you are not badly hurt, my lord."

"I will not die," he replied evenly, not bothering to correct Lisid's mode of address.

"It is only a sprained ankle. He should be well come the morning," Seona observed. "Nevertheless, the men were wise to keep the weight from it, or risk worse injury by riding. It was kind of Naoghas to assist him."

At the mention of her husband, Lisid's lip curled slightly. She glanced scornfully at Seona before smiling at Griffydd.

"I am so very glad to hear that your injury is not serious, my lord," she simpered, eyeing his limb in a way that made Griffydd feel that he might as well be naked—and he most definitely didn't want Lisid to see him naked.

The fact that he was wearing a *brat* made her bold scrutiny even more unwelcome.

"We should leave our guest in peace," Seona said, "so that he may rest."

"But did your father not command you to tend to me until I am well?" he reminded her.

"That will not be necessary," she answered firmly. "As I said, you will be better in the morning."

"I think we had best obey the chieftain's order," Griffydd persisted. "We would not want him to be angry."

Lisid made a sulky little frown and tossed her head. "I am not afraid of him!"

Griffydd looked taken aback. "Oh, I'm sure he pays little heed to you," he said matter-of-factly. "However, his daughter is no doubt another matter."

Seona could only smile in stunned gratitude for the kind remark while an angry frown marred Lisid's shallow beauty.

"He doesn't care about Seona at all!" Lisid declared. "And it would be a *disgrace* if she spent the night with you."

"Why would it be a disgrace?" Griffydd inquired coolly. "I am an honorable knight, as well as the guest of her father. Surely you are not implying I would ever take advantage of my host's daughter, or any other woman under his rule?"

"You wouldn't?" Lisid replied, obviously torn between the need to agree because of his conviction, and personal disappointment.

Although this was a bizarre and possibly distressing situation, Seona couldn't help enjoying Lisid's confused reactions.

"Indeed," Seona interjected. "I fear staying here will be a tedious chore. I would rather serve the cousin of King Haakon in the hall than sit here all night.''

It seemed to dawn on Lisid that their most recent visitor was also a notable man.

Seona gasped dramatically. ''That is no reflection on you, Sir Griffydd, of course.''

''I never get to see the important people anymore,'' Lisid muttered, pouting. ''Not since Fionn was born.''

''Alas for you,'' Griffydd sympathized solemnly.

''And them,'' Seona added gravely.

''I have an idea!'' Lisid cried, brightening. ''If I bring Fionn and Beitiris here, Seona, you can watch them and I may serve in the hall in your place.''

Seona stared, aghast. She had not anticipated this. ''Oh, I don't think—''

''By all means, bring the children here,'' Griffydd interrupted calmly.

Before Seona had another chance to protest this outrageous plan, Lisid had already dashed from the longhouse.

Leaving Seona alone with the far from incapacitated, handsome, chivalrous Griffydd DeLanyea, who seemingly preferred her to Lisid.

He rose from his bed.

''What are you doing?'' she demanded.

''God's wounds,'' he muttered, staring at his ankle. ''I think you broke my foot.''

''No, I didn't. I only banged it a little,'' she said, quite unrepentant considering what he had just arranged.

He gingerly sat back down. "I will have to remember that you are not a woman to be trifled with."

"No, I'm not," she replied, reminding herself at the same time. "And I don't think we should be alone together."

"Any more than we have already been?" he added helpfully.

"Yes!"

"We won't be alone," he reminded her. "The children will be here."

Seona didn't mask her displeasure at his rejoinder. "You should have accepted Lisid's offer to stay in my place. Indeed, most men would be only too happy to be alone with her, particularly when she is in such a *friendly* humor."

"I have known whores with more modesty," he muttered scornfully, lying down and pillowing his head on his hands.

It should have come as no shock that he had known whores. He was a virile man past his youth. He had probably been with all kinds of women.

Ignoring him, she searched for a lamp, because it was growing dark. She certainly did not want the lack of light to enfold them in intimate darkness.

"What are you looking for?"

"A lamp. It's getting dark."

"Ah. Would that not be a lamp hanging from the beam beside your head?"

She turned around so fast, it nearly hit her. "Oh.

Yes. Thank you,'' she snapped as she hurried to fill it and add a wick.

"I have known whores with more modesty, but I have not slept with them,'' he remarked.

Her fingers trembled as she struck a flint. "It would not matter to me if you had.''

"My foster brother finds them entertaining and sometimes insists on introducing me.''

She gave him a skeptical, sidelong glance before trying to light the lamp again. "I suppose you're a virgin, then.''

"No.''

Unsuccessful again, she almost threw down the flint and steel in frustration.

"Here, let me.''

He rose from the bed and held out his hand.

Without a word, she slapped the flint and steel into his palm and retreated, while he, with infuriating calm, lit the lamp.

When he turned to face her, he did not look triumphant. Instead, he looked at her with serious scrutiny.

He had not meant to upset her, and even though he had spoken the truth, he wished he had never said anything about Dylan's whores. "Why does everyone ignore you?''

"They don't,'' she retorted, his question obviously catching her off guard.

"They do. Naoghas did, Lisid did,'' he observed. "Yet you are their chieftain's daughter.''

"It does not trouble me," she said with a shrug of her shoulders.

She coughed a little as a puff of smoke coiled upward from the lamp. She hung it on the chain dangling from the beam before she stepped back into the dimness, where he could not see her so well. "I would rather they ignore me, and leave me alone."

"Ah!" he said, and sighed, understanding. He sometimes felt that way, too—and never more than when Dylan tried to entice him to share his "recreation."

Griffydd continued to regard Seona thoughtfully as she busied herself putting away the flint and steel and tidying the few articles of apparel he had left lying about before going on the hunt. He had never noticed the few freckles splashed across the bridge of her nose, like faerie kisses.

Nor had he realized how the hue of her hair varied with the light. Outside, in the bright daylight, it was almost fair, with a touch of red. Inside, in the dimness of his dwelling, it darkened to a ruddier color.

More like her full lips.

"Tell me, why does your father treat you as he does?"

"I would rather not talk about that," she said, wandering down the longhouse as if she had never been inside it before.

He didn't reply, and after a moment, she glanced back as he limped to a halt near her. "He is a fool if he does not see your merit, Seona,'' he said softly. Sincerely. Tenderly. ''They all are.''

Her brow contracted, she turned to face him, her gaze searching his face. ''Do you mean that? Do you truly mean that?''

''Yes, I do.''

He could see that she was still not willing to believe his assertion.

He wished he knew what he could say that would convince her. Perhaps words were not the way.

Then he realized, with shock and dismay, that she had started to cry. ''Seona, what it is?''

She sniffled and hiccuped like a little child as she tried to speak. ''I...I don't know...no one has ever...ever...''

At that moment, Fionn came tottering into the building.

Seona hastily wiped her face as she hurried toward the little boy.

Despite her tears, she had never felt so happy, so accepted, so respected. Griffydd DeLanyea liked her—*her,* so often scorned and ignored. She thought she might soar like a bird if she stepped outside.

She smiled as Fionn halted when he saw Griffydd, then promptly fell onto his bottom.

''Oh, come now, little man,'' the Welshman said in a gentle voice behind her, ''surely you are not afraid of me!''

Seona watched as Griffydd, wincing only a little, limped to the boy and squatted so that he was nearly nose to nose with the child. "We are friends, you and me."

Fionn nodded gravely, then reached out his arms. Griffydd scooped him up, returning Fionn's shy smile as he held the little boy in his strong arms.

It was not as Griffydd had smiled at her that first moment, Seona realized, although his expression now was a kind, friendly smile nearly as attractive. It was a fatherly smile, or so she had always imagined a loving father would smile at a beloved child.

A type of smile her own had never made for her.

Lisid appeared on the threshold, holding a wiggling Beitiris against her shoulder. Her brows raised at the sight of her son in the Welshman's arms.

"Greetings, Lisid," Griffydd said, before turning his attention back to the boy. "Come, Fionn, I have something to show you." He sat the boy on the bed. "Something I have had a long time."

"Here, take Beitiris," Lisid said briskly to Seona. "I've fed her, but she won't settle." She glanced at Griffydd, then her son. "They seem to get along."

"Yes, they do," Seona agreed.

Lisid's eyes narrowed slightly. "Perhaps I should stay and you should serve in the hall."

"If you would rather," Seona replied. "I would like to hear the news from Haakon's court."

Lisid looked again at Griffydd, who paid her no heed, then handed Seona the baby. "I will try to return as soon as I can."

With that, and without a word of farewell to Fionn, Lisid ducked beneath the covering and was gone.

Seona turned to see what the Welshman and Fionn were doing, noticing that Fionn barely attended to his mother's departure.

Then she saw that Fionn held a wooden horse about a hand span tall. It was on a wooden base, and the base had wheels that Fionn turned, clearly fascinated.

"There is more," the Welshman said.

He upended the horse and pulled a panel from its belly. Inside the carved toy were five very small wooden soldiers, wonderfully made.

Beitiris began to cry. Griffydd and Fionn looked at her while Seona lightly and briskly patted the baby's back. "She just needs to burp, I'm sure."

Fionn frowned studiously. "Did the horse eat the men?" he inquired gravely.

Griffydd shook his head. "No, this is supposed to be the Trojan horse."

"What's that?" Fionn asked.

Seona didn't know what kind of horse he meant, either, and she hoped Beitiris would soon quiet so that she could hear the Welshman's explanation.

In an effort to do that, she started to bounce the baby, as well as pat her back.

Griffydd handed the horse back to Fionn, who tried to fit the soldiers inside it.

"Careful!" Seona cautioned. "Don't break them!"

"He won't," Griffydd said.

She had to strain to hear him over the sobbing baby

as he continued. "They are well made. They have survived me, and my brother, and my foster brother, and if Dylan didn't destroy them, nobody could."

Fionn looked smugly at Seona, then returned to his task. "I can't get the last one in," he complained.

Seona added rocking to bouncing and patting, and she felt the sweat from her exertions trickle down her sides.

"You will," Griffydd said, making no move to help him, showing rather surprising patience and restraint. Most men Seona knew would have snatched the toy away and shown him.

Griffydd gave her a questioning, sidelong glance that, Seona thought, seemed rather critical. "Have you never heard a baby cry?" she asked rather peevishly.

"Once or twice," he remarked with infuriating calm. He rose, and she noticed that he didn't seem to find his sore ankle as bothersome as before. "Let me hold her."

"Oh, I don't think so," she began reluctantly.

"I did it!" Fionn cried triumphantly. "Now tell me about the Trojan horse!"

Griffydd glanced at the boy over his shoulder. "When the baby settles down," he said. He faced Seona again. "Will you let me hold her while Fionn shows you the horse?"

There was a gentleness in his expression that reassured her, and a yearning in his eyes that compelled her. She carefully handed him Beitiris, ready to take her back at the first sign of a problem.

His weight on his left leg, Griffydd laid the baby against his muscular chest and proceeded to rub her back with a relaxed circular motion. Keeping a wary eye on them, Seona sat beside Fionn on the bed.

"See, look!" Fionn said proudly. "You open the belly like this and they come out."

As the wooden soldiers came tumbling out of the toy, Beitiris did one of the loudest burps Seona had ever heard from a baby. The infant immediately grew quiet, laying her downy head on the warrior's chest as if it belonged there.

Griffydd looked at Seona with a frustratingly inscrutable expression. "You were jostling her too much, I fear."

"Oh," Seona said, sounding pert and petty even to herself. She got up and approached him. "I'll take her now."

She put her hands around Beitiris to remove her, all the while trying not to think about her fingers brushing Griffydd's chest.

The baby uttered a wail of protest.

Seona looked up into Griffydd's gray eyes and, instead of dismay, thought she saw a twinkle of pleasure.

"I gather she wants to stay where she is," he observed. He started to rub her back once more and Beitiris stopped fussing immediately, again resting her head on his chest.

"Oh," Seona mumbled as she watched his long fingers move.

"This is no bother," he said softly, a sparkle of undeniable merriment in the depths of his eyes. "Women are the least trouble at this age."

Seona didn't want to smile, but she couldn't help it. "Men, too," she answered.

"Tell me about the horse!" the persistent Fionn demanded.

"Fionn!" Seona warned, going toward him. "This man is a guest here."

"A guest who will be happy to tell you the tale," the Welshman answered.

"Perhaps you would care for a drink before you begin?" Seona offered, ignoring Fionn's restless pluck at her sleeve. "I will pour you some wine. Or there is water." She gestured toward a bucket of fresh water in the corner.

"I am quite fine," he replied. He glanced at the little boy. "My audience is getting anxious."

Seona nodded her acquiescence and sat beside Fionn, who held on to the wooden horse.

"You know what I like to do when someone is telling me a story, Fionn?" Griffydd asked. "I like to lie down with my eyes closed, so I can imagine it all as he speaks. Why don't you do that?"

Seona was very impressed with his suggestion, for the hour was late and the children really should have been asleep. She knew if she had told Fionn to lie down, he would have protested vigorously. Instead, still clutching the wooden horse, he quickly laid his head on the goosedown pillow. "I'm ready," he prompted.

The Welshman, his expression very serious indeed, nodded. "Once, there were two kings who made war upon each other," he began in his fine, deep voice, one hand on the back of Beitiris's head. "And the war lasted for ten long years...."

Seona listened to him tell the tale of the siege and defeat of Troy with avid interest. Griffydd DeLanyea was a marvelous storyteller, never making things too complex, or too simple, either. Valiant Hector, petulant Achilles, weak-willed Helen and her lover Paris, who always seemed to be miraculously whisked out of battle into Helen's arms, came to life as he talked.

When the story drew to its dramatic finish, she wished he could begin all over again. So pleased was she that she lifted her hands to clap—only to have Griffydd quickly put his finger to his lips.

"You'll wake the young warrior," he admonished in a whisper.

She turned to see that Fionn, the horse in his arms, had fallen asleep. "Oh." She looked at Beitiris. "She's fast asleep, too."

In the next moment's silence, they both could hear the sounds of men singing coming from the hall. She had not noticed the noise while Griffydd was telling his story.

"Lisid may be some time yet," she noted anxiously, rising. "Your arms must be tired."

"A little," he admitted. He limped toward the bed. "I shall lay her here, on the other side of her brother. Then she cannot roll out."

He did so, and she watched as he covered both slumbering children with one of the blankets.

"I'm sorry we have commandeered your quarters like this. I could take the children to Lisid's house and wait for her there," she offered.

He regarded her steadily, with a spark of something that was not merriment smoldering in his solemn eyes.

"But then you would not be obeying your father's orders," he said in his enticing voice. "You are to tend me until I am well."

Chapter Nine

Seona swallowed hard.

The flame of the lamp began to sputter.

"It's going out," she cried softly, not wanting to wake the children, glad of the excuse to turn away and collect her thoughts, which seemed as scattered as the sparks in a smithy.

She also felt as hot as if she stood beside a forge.

"There is more oil somewhere," she said.

"I'll help you look."

"No, no, please, sit!"

Mercifully he did just that, sitting on the chest.

She began to search the corners of the hut, seeking the clay jar containing whale oil. "Ah, here it is!"

She carefully lowered the lamp and added to the oil, biting her lip to keep her hand steady.

"Now where will *you* sit?" he asked solemnly.

"I...perhaps we should go."

"Why disobey your father? Do you not feel safe here?"

"Of course I do," she retorted, crossing her arms over her chest.

"I am glad to hear it." He smiled a little. "I would enjoy the company."

"Oh." She went to the end of the bed and sat gingerly on the edge.

"Your friend has fine children," the Welshman noted matter-of-factly, crossing his arms over his broad chest as he regarded her steadily. "Strong and healthy."

"Yes, yes, she does," Seona replied, looking at them. "You may have quite a time getting that horse away from Fionn."

Griffydd responded with a shrug. "I will have to give him something in trade perhaps."

"Tell me, do you always carry a toy with you to amuse children?"

"That one I do," he replied. "My father made it for me before I was born, and I carry it to remind me of home."

"But your father is a baron," she said wonderingly. She truly could not imagine a man of wealth and power taking the time or the care to make a child's toy, even if the child was his firstborn son and heir.

"He is a man of many skills."

"I see. Like you."

The Welshman smiled very slowly, and it seemed to envelope her in a warmth of companionship and intimacy. "You think I possess many skills?"

"You are surely a fine warrior," she said as evenly as she could. "You must have some skill at negotiating, if your father sends you on this mission. You have a lovely voice for singing, and you are a wonderful storyteller."

"You had best take care, Seona, or I could grow vain," he replied softly.

She made a wry smile. "Or I could, if you truly prefer my company to Lisid's."

"Seona, there is something I would understand, if I could," he said quietly, his gaze seeming to grow more intense. "Why are you so little respected here?"

Because of his kindness toward her and the genuine concern in his expression, she answered him.

"My father does not like me," she confessed. "He never has, from the day I was born and was not a son. And then I was a sickly infant. The others only emulate him."

Griffydd continued to regard her steadily, as if he somehow knew there must be more.

"When I was about Fionn's age, my mother ran off with another man."

"What happened to her?"

Seona shook her head and stared at her entwined fingers in her lap. "I don't know."

He rose and came to kneel before her, gently cupping her face so that she had to look into his serious eyes. "But you are not to blame for any of those things," he said softly.

"I know," she said in a whisper as tortured as her

eyes. "Yet is it so strange that a chieftain would want a fine, healthy son for his firstborn?"

And then he saw something that completely tore at his heart: shame.

"If I had been a boy...or pretty..."

He jumped to his feet and pulled her trembling body into his arms, embracing her, trying as best he could to comfort her.

"Seona," he whispered fervently. "Seona, you are perfect as you are."

As she quietly sobbed and clung to him, he silently raged at Diarmad MacMurdoch, who was so harsh to Seona and made her doubt her value, as well as the mother who would abandon her. Why, Seona was worth a hundred like Lisid! Indeed, there was no finer woman in all the world.

She gently extricated herself from his embrace, wiping her damp face on her sleeve.

"I am sorry," she said, and he knew she was trying to smile. "I should not be weak and foolish."

"I do not think you cry often."

She took a deep breath and shook her head. "No, I do not."

"You are an admirable woman, Seona."

"Am I? Not tonight, I fear."

She went to the door and peered outside. "They are still singing," she murmured. "And not well, either. That must be difficult for a Welshman to bear."

She turned back to him and made a little smile, and he knew it was for him alone.

He could control his desire no longer. He went to her and, taking her gently by her shoulders, bent to kiss her—

"I'm thirsty!"

Seona and Griffydd sprang apart as if Fionn's announcement had been a battle cry.

Seona didn't dare glance at Griffydd as she flushed with guilty embarrassment to think what Fionn might have witnessed in another few moments.

Not that she was ashamed of that, necessarily, or her feelings. But explanations might have been necessary, and she could hardly offer the child a truthful one.

She hurried toward the bed. "Let me get you a drink of water."

"No!" Fionn grumbled, rubbing his sleepy eyes. "I want *him* to get it!"

"But he is our guest and—"

"And I will be happy to oblige," Griffydd said behind her, and she heard the subtle undertone of frustration. No doubt she heard it because she felt the same.

"You must speak softly, Fionn," Seona admonished as she heard Griffydd fill the goblet with water from the bucket. "We don't want to wake Beitiris."

As if her words had been a signal, the baby began to cry. Seona gently lifted the infant and held her in her arms, rocking slowly, while Griffydd limped to the bed and offered Fionn the water.

The little boy gulped his drink as if he had been wandering in the desert for a fortnight, while Seona noted with relief that Beitiris had fallen back to sleep. When Fionn was finished, he thrust the goblet at Griffydd.

"Say thank you," Seona reminded him.

"Thank you. Now tell me another story."

"Fionn!"

Griffydd chuckled. "I will, if you lie down and keep still so that your sister can sleep."

"I don't want to lie down," Fionn mumbled grumpily. "I'm not sleepy."

"Fionn, the hour is late and—"

"And I'm not sleepy," he declared, startling the baby into wakefulness.

"Here, then, sit on my knee," Griffydd offered, taking a seat on the chest and patting his lap. "I will tell you a story if you sit here quietly."

Fionn considered a moment.

"All right," he conceded. He jumped down from the bed and hurried over to the warrior, climbing onto his lap as if there were nothing at all extraordinary about this situation.

"Tell me about a knight and a dragon—but no girls!" he commanded.

"No girls?" Griffydd inquired solemnly.

Fionn shook his head. "No. A girl would be too scared of a dragon."

Griffydd gave Seona a sidelong glance, his eyes shining. "Some would, but a few would not."

"I don't believe that!"

"Someday you might, although girls of such bold spirit are very rare, indeed."

"I don't want a girl in my story!" Fionn insisted, pouting as only a sleepy three-year-old can.

"Very well. No girls," Griffydd conceded.

Seona had to stifle a smile, for she could tell that the Welshman was hard put to keep a straight face.

The baby was asleep, so she carefully laid Beitiris on the bed, only to see her open her eyes. She picked up the baby again and rocked some more.

Fionn poked Griffydd in the chest. "Start!"

Once more Beitiris slumbered, so again Seona laid her down—and again the baby's eyes opened.

"Why don't you lie beside her? That might help to settle her," Griffydd suggested. "She will be warmer that way, will she not?" His expression changed, and his voice dropped into a low, husky timbre. "I know I would like that."

Seona flushed hotly and lay down on the bed—*his* bed, although she tried not to think about that—and snuggled the baby in her arms.

Fionn tugged on the neck of Griffydd's *chroich.* "Tell me my story!"

As Griffydd obeyed, Seona realized he was right. Warm in Seona's arms, the baby soon fell asleep.

The bed was very comfortable, and it was cozy there in the dimly lit longhouse, with Fionn comfortably ensconced on Griffydd's lap and the Welshman's soothing voice telling a tale of a knight on a crusade who got left behind by his king and had to fight a terrible dragon named Cynric before he could go home.

Seona yawned and her eyes drifted closed.

The last thing she saw before she fell asleep was Fionn nestled against the Welshman's broad chest as if he belonged there, and her last thought was that Griffydd DeLanyea would make a wonderful father.

The hour grew late. Several of Diarmad's warriors slumbered where they sat. Others, like Naoghas and his friends, talked in hushed voices, drank ale and nibbled at the remains of the food, which Lisid and a few other women waited to clear away.

Naoghas glanced often at his wife, who ignored him. She concentrated instead on the chieftain and his important guest.

"I thought the son of Baron DeLanyea was also in Dunloch," Olaf suddenly remarked, his voice considerably lower than it had been all night.

Diarmad realized this was intended to be a confidential discussion. "He is. He has come to make some arrangements for the transportation of his father's goods. Unfortunately, he fell from his horse and hurt his ankle. My daughter tends to him."

Olaf turned a suspicious eye onto Diarmad. "*She* tends to him?"

Diarmad's expression was bland as he uttered a smooth combination of falsehoods and truths. "She is skilled in such matters. And like his father, this man lives and breathes honor and trustworthiness. I would even allow him access to my money—if I possessed much.''

And if he seduced Seona, Diarmad thought with greedy satisfaction, they would have to marry. Seona would finally be truly useful, for he would have an unbreakable alliance with Baron DeLanyea, whom all men feared and respected.

Let Haakon think about *that!*

''I am sure both are trustworthy,'' Olaf replied. ''It would be different if she looked like *her,*'' he continued, nodding at the woman who seemed to realize they were discussing her, even if she couldn't hear their words.

Diarmad frowned. Lisid had caused no end of trouble among his warriors ever since she grew breasts. He had hoped her marriage would put an end to the conflicts over her favors. Unfortunately, this had not happened.

He would have sent her away, except that Lisid came to his bed, too. Nobody knew of it, of course, and he had warned Lisid that she would regret it if she revealed their liaison. So far, his threats and her enjoyment of his occasional presents had guaranteed her silence.

''She is a very beautiful woman,'' Olaf remarked significantly.

''Lisid is also a married woman,'' Diarmad said, guessing what Olaf wanted.

Not even the cousin of a king could insist upon a married woman to keep him company.

Olaf frowned as he stretched and belched. "Diarmad, I thank you for the fine meal," he said, rising. "Now it is time I slept."

"You are welcome to share the hospitality of my hall," Diarmad offered.

The Norseman shook his head. "Again my thanks, but I prefer to sleep in my tent."

Diarmad had expected him to say that and, in truth, he was relieved not to have the man spend more time in his hall than strictly necessary. Although his personal wealth was well concealed, a Norseman of Olaf's age and experience could probably sniff it out, then demand a share for his silence.

"Will you walk with me to my tent?" Olaf asked.

Diarmad had no desire to set foot outside his hall on a cold night; unfortunately, Olaf was an important guest, so Diarmad, wrapping his black bear robe around him, lumbered to his feet. "Of course."

He hoped the Norseman appreciated the gesture.

The two men sauntered out of the hall, neither one of them acknowledging Lisid as they went out into the night.

The stars and quarter moon shone down on them, lighting their way. Out of habit, Diarmad sniffed the air. He detected no hint of a change of weather.

A dog barked in the distance, and as they walked toward the group of tents set up in the meadow beside the fortress, they could hear the occasional murmur from the longhouses between the fortress and the wharf.

The two men said nothing, each wrapped in his own thoughts, until they reached the Norse encampment.

The tops of the braced frames of the tents were carved in the shape of dragons' heads, like the prows of their longships. Heavy woolen coverings hung over a pole suspended between the frames. In the center of the camp, a large cauldron hung on a tripod over an open fire. The glow from the flickering flames made the tents look like a herd of dragons at rest.

It occurred to Diarmad that these Norsemen were like such mystical creatures: temporarily somnambulant, but capable of great destruction if they were roused. He would have to tread carefully around Olaf, especially with the Welshman in their midst.

Olaf spoke softly to a man who was apparently merely sitting beside a small fire smoldering outside the first tent they came to; Diarmad had no doubts the man was really a sentry.

He did not fault the Norsemen. Indeed, the one time he had gone to see Haakon in person, he, too, had set watchmen outside his camp. It was only wise, whether those around you were supposedly friends or definitely foes.

Olaf strode toward the largest tent and held back the flap for Diarmad to enter.

Enter the dragon's lair? Diarmad thought with

some dismay. Here, surrounded by the crew of the Norse longship?

Yet what would Olaf make of a refusal?

Putting his hand on the hilt of his dagger, as if afraid it would catch on the tent fabric and not to reassure himself of its comforting presence, Diarmad entered.

Olaf followed him into the tent. A brass oil lamp on a slender stand had been stuck into the ground, providing light. There was also a carved bed, smaller than one a jarl would have in his home, covered with furs and sporting a goosedown pillow. A bossed box stood near its head, and a finely carved chair completed the furnishings.

All of them proved that Olaf was a man of wealth and standing among his people.

Olaf gestured toward the chair, and Diarmad sat while Olaf poured some wine into a drinking horn. He handed it to Diarmad, then half sat, half reclined on the bed.

"I wanted to speak to you in private," the jarl announced.

As he nodded, Diarmad noted that Olaf had not given himself any wine.

"The king is very concerned about your possible alliance with the DeLanyeas," Olaf said bluntly.

This was not unexpected.

"It is a trade pact, nothing more," Diarmad assured him.

"A pact with one of the most powerful barons in

Wales, and a man whose daughter has recently wed the brother-in-law of Etienne DeGuerre, one of the most influential Norman barons in England," Olaf replied. "What kind of trade do you discuss?"

"The Welshman has silver and wool he needs shipped. I am to provide the men and ships to carry it, for which I will receive a share of the profits," Diarmad explained.

"How much?"

Diarmad stifled his displeasure at the Norseman's arrogant tone and impertinent questions. While not of equal rank with a jarl, he was a chieftain and leader of a village. This man might have the right to question him, but not with such impudence. "The amount of the share is what Griffydd DeLanyea is here to discuss, as well as the number of ships I will put at their disposal."

The Norseman nodded, but his suspicious expression did not alter. "You plan no formal alliance? You do not seek an alliance through marriage between your daughter and Baron DeLanyea's son?"

"Griffydd DeLanyea is a Welshman with Norman blood," Diarmad said, feigning surprise as if the thought of a marriage had never entered his head, or if it had, that there were serious obstacles to such a union. "All I seek is profit, not alliances."

"Don't try to trick me," Olaf warned. "I know what kind of scheming man you are, Diarmad. A union between you and that family would give you great power. But I can respect your desire. So can Haakon, which is why I have been sent.''

"I thought you came for the scatt.''

"That, and to warn you that Haakon will not look favorably upon a marriage between your family and the DeLanyeas. Haakon hopes you will not forget where your true allegiance belongs.''

Diarmad subdued the urge to scowl. He had been ignored for years by Haakon and his jarls; now, when he was on the brink of gaining some small measure of influence with the Welsh and the Normans, too, Haakon sent his cousin to stop him.

But if Haakon thought a marriage between Seona and DeLanyea meant a conspiracy against him, Diarmad had little choice but to abandon the idea, or Haakon would send his ships to attack Dunloch. They would descend on his village like a pack of wolves.

Diarmad shrugged as if to say that while he could not disagree, he did not think Olaf's words applied in this case.

"You had better not give Haakon any reason to doubt your loyalty.''

This time, Diarmad could not completely stifle his annoyance at the man's insolent words.

"What have I to show for my allegiance to Haakon?'' he retorted. "All he does is demand more scatt from me and my people, and then send his jarls to threaten me when I try to earn the money to pay it.''

"You are not a stupid man, Diarmad,'' Olaf replied, "and I am sure you have heard that there are those seeking to overthrow Haakon, your rightful overlord. If he demands your money, it is because he must protect his kingdom—which is also yours."

Diarmad scowled. "My kingdom is here, not in the north."

Olaf's eyes narrowed. "So you would desert Haakon and throw your allegiance to the Welsh, or do you plan to support the king of the Scots?"

"King of the Scots? Do I look daft, man?" Diarmad retorted. "Which one? Every man who sports the *brat* claims to be the rightful heir to the Scots throne." He shook his head. "No, I would not be so stupid as to get involved with those hotheads. It is all I can do to keep them away from my land and out of my business."

"And a good business you have, too." Olaf's eyes gleamed with the pleasure of revealing a secret. "I suppose you have built a fleet of longships to protect yourself from the Scots?"

Diarmad nearly fell out of the chair. "Longships?"

"Are you denying you have them?"

Diarmad thought quickly, and quickly came to the conclusion that somehow Olaf, if not Haakon, knew of his fleet and it would not be wise to dissemble. Otherwise, Olaf would surely report that Diarmad was conspiring against him with the Scots or the Welsh or both.

"I have made no secret of my fleet," he lied. "The king had but to ask how many ships I command."

"Ah, it is the king's fault he is ignorant of your ships?" Olaf queried. "Or was it that one of his jarls had to see them for himself?"

Diarmad wanted to growl with frustration. He had thought the bay he had chosen well-hidden—or else he had a spy in his midst who had told the king of his fleet.

That had to be it, for how else could Olaf know about his beautiful longships?

When he found out who had told the Norsemen of his fleet, Diarmad silently vowed, he would have the man drowned very slowly in a tidal pool.

"So, you have warships," Olaf continued. "When Haakon is told, and of course it is my duty to inform him of what I have seen, he will demand an increase in the scatt, at the very least."

Diarmad frowned, thinking of the tribute he already paid.

"If I marry your daughter, I am sure he could be persuaded otherwise."

Chapter Ten

Diarmad stared at the Norseman, dumbfounded.

"Haakon wants me to wed your daughter," Olaf announced.

It was obvious that while Olaf was willing to comply with this plan, he was not pleased, for he looked as if he had tasted bad fish.

Not that Diarmad cared a whit what Olaf thought, for he felt as if he had won a great prize.

He had hoped that when word of Seona's marriage to DeLanyea reached the king, Haakon would finally stop treating him like a beggar at the gates.

But now, without that, Haakon was proposing a union with the royal family! His homely, useless daughter was to be betrothed to the cousin of Haakon!

What was a marriage into the family of a Welsh-Norman baron compared to that?

Obviously Haakon feared an alternate alliance. He, Diarmad MacMurdoch of Dunloch, had the upper hand at last!

Yet he would not betray any enthusiasm for a marriage between Seona and Olaf, at least not now. That way, perhaps he could reduce the scatt a considerable amount.

"Naturally I'm flattered that the king wishes to join his house to my own," Diarmad replied modestly, "but surely we are unworthy."

The look that passed over Olaf's face revealed that he thought that, too. Nevertheless, he made a somewhat strained smile.

"If Haakon believed that, he would never have proposed it," he replied. "Of course you are worthy. Chieftain of a village and a shrewd fellow." He paused a moment. "And your daughter is beautiful. She will be a fine bride."

Diarmad felt some small pity for Olaf's situation. He, too, had been forced to wed a woman not of his choosing. But what was Olaf's displeasure compared to what *he* was going to gain?

"Is there not a dowry of five hundred pieces of silver?" Olaf asked after a moment.

Some of Diarmad's delight dissipated, and he wished he had cut out his tongue before he had made that drunken offer to a princeling from the Isle of Man last year. Fortunately, the fellow had gotten himself killed in a raid on Ireland before a betrothal could be agreed upon.

Diarmad had sworn that he would never again get that drunk when entertaining unmarried male visitors.

"If the king favors the match, surely the dowry can be…discussed," he prevaricated.

"I think you overestimate the king's enthusiasm for this marriage, Diarmad."

The beefy Norseman leaned forward, so that his face shone in the glow of the lamplight. "He is not the one in immediate danger of being accused of being a traitor to his king. He is not the one who has raised a large fleet without his overlord's knowledge. He is not the one who is negotiating with powerful foreigners. I should think you would consider yourself lucky to be restored to the king's favor with your scatt unchanged, as well as get rid of your skinny daughter, for a mere five hundred pieces of silver. Now, will you agree to this betrothal and dowry, or not?"

Diarmad thought of his fine and expensive longships and knew one day Haakon would find a way to take some of them away, unless he was clever. The one possibility to prevent that, or at least delay it, was to have an ally in the royal house. If that ally was a son-in-law, so much the better.

"Very well," he replied slowly. "I will give you my daughter in marriage and her dowry will be five hundred pieces of silver." He spit on his hand and held it out to the Norseman.

Olaf stared at Diarmad's open palm, then said, "You would clasp hands tonight?"

Diarmad gave the man a suspicious look. "Why not? I have agreed to the marriage. What prevents you from making the betrothal binding?"

"My word alone should be enough."

"Or do you need Haakon's approval first?" Diarmad proposed, purposefully making it sound as if he suspected Olaf lacked the authority to make the promise, instead needing to sail back to Haakon like a child seeking approval from its mother.

"No, I do not!" the Norseman declared sourly.

He also spit into his palm. Then he clasped hands with the father of his future bride.

Diarmad got to his feet. "Olaf, since this is a concluded bargain between us, and neither you nor Haakon now have cause to doubt my loyalty, I see no reason I cannot also make the bargain with the Welshman. Indeed, I'll need that agreement if I'm to raise the five hundred pieces of silver."

Olaf nodded his concurrence.

"Yet I fear young DeLanyea is a cautious fellow. The news of this betrothal might make him think he needs to consult with his father, since I will be more closely tied to Haakon after your marriage. I think it would be better, then, if this decision remained between the two of us until DeLanyea and I come to terms."

"Very well," Olaf replied with another nod.

"I see you are a wise man, Olaf." Diarmad cleared his throat and looked at the sides of the tent as he stroked his beard. "It might be better not to tell Seona about this betrothal for the present, either."

"Why do you say that?" the Norseman demanded, suddenly wary. "Will she not do as you command?"

"Of course she will!" Diarmad replied quickly. "But you know women! She will surely be so delighted and flattered, she will never be able to keep it a secret."

Olaf relaxed. "Of course. As you wish."

Diarmad went to the threshold of the tent and turned back to face Olaf, the lamplight and shadows making his face eerie.

"I hardly expected such honors when I saw your ship in my harbor," he said. He bowed slightly. "I leave you to your rest, son-in-law."

Disgruntled and thinking of the sacrifices men must make for their king, the Norseman made an answering inclination of his head, then watched the chieftain duck under the flap and disappear from view.

"Sleep well, Diarmad," he muttered before reaching for Diarmad's wine.

The canny old chieftain had not so much as sipped it. There was no sense letting the expensive wine go to waste.

The tent flap moved again. Olaf looked up, wondering what more Diarmad had to say.

But it was not Diarmad who came into his tent.

Griffydd sighed softly and shifted his shoulders, trying to find a more comfortable position for his back against the stone wall. When that did not prove possible, he resigned himself to remaining as still as he could while Fionn continued to slumber, his small body on Griffydd's lap and his head against Griffydd's chest.

The lamp was burning out, too. Well, he could not do anything about that at the moment. In the meantime, he would content himself watching Seona sleep, the baby snuggled against her as if she belonged there.

A surge of longing rose in his breast, like a long-suppressed appetite whetted by the scent of fresh bread. How much he wanted a child of his own! It would be the greatest gift a woman could ever give him, a source of boundless joy and love. An excuse, perhaps, to love unabashedly and to express that love in a way he never could with women.

Or thought he never could.

Now, as he regarded Seona, he wondered if it had only been that he had never found the woman who was capable of rousing the desire to express his feelings, or to make him love with his whole heart.

He could almost hear his heart expand at that thought, and then the next: that if she could be his wife and bear his children, he would surely know pure happiness.

Lisid slipped beneath the woolen cloth and into the longhouse, her face lit by the rushlight she carried. Flushed and somewhat flustered, her gaze ran over the scene before her. Then she smiled with obvious satisfaction.

"Oh, forgive me, my lord!" she exclaimed softly and, he thought, quite insincerely, while she set the torch in the wall sconce. "I didn't mean to be so long, but I thought it best to wait until my husband was asleep before I fetched the children." Her contrite expression changed to a peevish frown. "That way, he wouldn't disturb them when he came stumbling home stinking of ale."

"I have had longer watches than this," Griffydd whispered in reply. He rose slowly and carefully, still holding Fionn.

"And of course you and Seona could be trusted to attend to the children."

His eyes narrowed slightly. "What do you mean?"

She gave him another sly smile. "Why, that there was no chance you would neglect them for...other things."

"In that, you are quite right," he snapped, disliking Lisid intensely, for he could tell what she was thinking—that Seona was hardly a woman to inspire passion.

It was very tempting to tell Lisid exactly how he felt about Seona, yet the woman obviously cared about little beyond her own vanity. She certainly didn't see how annoyed he was.

"I fear you will have to carry Fionn home for me, if you are able," she whispered coyly, "or we shall have to wake him."

Griffydd glanced down at the little boy he held against his chest, then nodded. "I will manage it."

"I'll wake Seona," Lisid said.

Griffydd swiftly limped in front of her.

"Let her sleep," he commanded, the words an order even though he whispered. "Take the baby. I will wake Seona when I return."

For an instant, it looked as if Lisid contemplated protesting, but she glanced at his face and wisely reconsidered. Instead, she gently lifted Beitiris without disturbing Seona.

Pouting a little, she took the rushlight from the sconce and led the way out of the longhouse.

As they went toward Lisid's house, Griffydd surveyed the Norse encampment. It was large, befitting the crew of the sizable longship tied to the wharf.

He wondered what had really brought a Norse nobleman to Dunloch, and more than half suspected *his* arrival was at least partly responsible. Tomorrow, he would meet this unexpected visitor and try to gauge how the jarl's presence would affect the trade negotiations.

At the very least, wily old Diarmad would be distracted.

Which could mean that the negotiations might take some time to conclude.

That would have disturbed Griffydd when he first arrived, but now it made him smile inwardly with delight.

Seona rolled over, then woke with a start, for Beitiris was not beside her. She sat up and scanned the longhouse.

She quickly realized she was alone.

Where had Griffydd gone, and why had he taken the children?

She jumped to her feet and ran to the door, hurrying outside. Her panicked gaze searched the village, coming to rest when she saw a man come out of Lisid's longhouse, followed by Lisid herself.

Of course! she thought with a sigh of relief. He had helped Lisid take the children home.

She watched as Lisid put a cloak over Griffydd's shoulders, and she recognized the black garment she had last seen wrapped around a wet Fionn.

They spoke together, their bodies nearly touching, their faces close.

And then Lisid raised herself on her toes and kissed him.

Taken aback by the woman's kiss and disgusted with her wanton manner, Griffydd pushed her away. "What are you doing, woman?" he demanded scornfully.

"Thanking you," she said in a low, lascivious voice.

"I do not want such thanks."

Her eyes widened with disbelief. "You—?"

"Go inside to your husband and children," he ordered.

With a toss of her pretty head, she turned on her heel and obeyed.

Griffydd, too angry to pay much heed to his sore foot, marched toward the guest quarters, his cloak swinging about his ankles with his angry strides. God's wounds, he had thought Lisid understood that he was not interested in her in any way. First, she was not Seona. Secondly, she was a married woman.

Unfortunately, with a woman of Lisid's ilk, he could not be certain she comprehended his aversion to her kiss, even if she had reacted with indignation when he ordered her to get back inside with her husband.

He entered the longhouse, expecting to find Seona still asleep. Instead, she stood beside the lamp, eyeing him quizzically.

A curse flew to Griffydd's lips. He hoped she had not seen Lisid kiss him!

"You're not asleep," he observed somewhat cautiously, removing the cloak and laying it over the chest.

"Obviously. You should have awakened me when Lisid came for the children."

"Yes, I should," he agreed, feeling rather like an errant schoolboy facing his tutor, if his tutor had been a very desirable young woman. "Are you angry with me?"

"Why would I be?"

She must not have witnessed Lisid's horrible kiss, he thought with relief. "That woman should be muzzled," he muttered.

Seona's brow furrowed. "Did Lisid say something to insult you, or is it the kiss you did not like?"

He glanced at her sharply. "You did see!"

"Oh, yes," she replied lightly, and he thought her nonchalance genuine. "I would not make much of that. She kisses anybody who wears a *brat*. She sleeps with just about everybody, too."

Although he was relieved that Seona was not upset, he was aggravated nonetheless. "Well, I do not!"

"No?"

"No!"

"Yet you have known whores with more modesty."

Griffydd's eyes widened with surprise, then he flushed hotly beneath her steadfast gaze. "I do not claim to be without fault, but I did not want her to kiss me!"

Her gaze faltered for a moment as she smiled a little, then shook her head. "Poor Naoghas," she murmured sympathetically. "I fear he was so flattered when she accepted him, he never considered what marriage with her would truly be like."

"Lisid should be punished for such behavior!" Griffydd said sternly. "I am surprised your father allows it."

"You should not be, for Lisid shares her favors with him, too, although he thinks nobody knows about it." She gave Griffydd a wry look. "I think that's why Naoghas doesn't do anything. He fears Diarmad will take her side over his."

"Would he?"

Seona grew somber. "Or he might prefer that nobody knows of his liaison with one of his warrior's wives and so claim she is lying. I cannot be sure what he would do, any more than Naoghas can be.''

''Perhaps Naoghas feels it is wiser to swallow his pride than risk greater shame, as you did the first night I was here when your father ordered you to escort me to my quarters,'' he suggested.

''You think I swallowed my pride? Perhaps I don't possess any.''

He smiled slowly. ''Now who is the liar?''

Suddenly the lamp went out, sending them into pitch-blackness. Waiting for her eyes to get used to the dark, Seona didn't move, afraid if she did, she would collide with him.

Instead, he walked into her, nearly knocking her off her feet.

''Forgive me!'' he quietly cried, steadying her.

She tried to ignore the sensation of his hands on her, although his touch seemed to set her afire with longing. ''I will find the flint and steel and more oil in a moment, when I can see better.''

''Perhaps I should stay right where I am,'' he said softly, his hands still on her arms. ''I might knock you down, or hurt myself. Of course, then you would have to tend to me longer, so that would not be so bad.''

She swallowed hard. ''I think you do not have to keep holding on to me, unless your ankle is still weak.''

''There is that, too,'' he murmured.

Aware that he was not behaving like an honorable

guest by continuing to stand so close to her, inhaling the delightful fragrance of sun and grass and pine that seemed to emanate from her, he let go and watched as she found flint and steel, refilled and lit the lamp.

If he were wise, he would tell her to go without delay.

If he were wise, or older, or less enamored of her, perhaps.

"Are you trembling?" she asked suddenly.

He realized he was. "I fear I am not used to this *brat,*" he replied, although he knew the chill on his legs was only a part of the reason.

"I will light a fire, too," she offered.

"I would prefer to warm myself another way," he whispered as he gently pulled her into his embrace.

She made no effort to refuse and that delighted him.

"This is...this is very warm, indeed," she murmured, laying her head against his chest, nestling against him as if she belonged there.

She did belong there and, by her action, she told him she thought so, too.

He laughed softly with the delight that realization gave him, his chest vibrating against her cheek.

"What amuses you so?" she asked softly.

"It is not amusement that is making me laugh, Seona," he whispered as he bent his head to kiss her. "It is joy."

She welcomed his kiss with eager ardor and it

deepened as his hands entwined themselves in her hair, just as he had longed to do.

Moaning, she leaned against him. He could feel her breasts, her hips, her knees—and he wanted more.

He thrust his tongue between her soft lips while his hands explored her body.

He had never felt this way about a woman, that he must know every inch of her. Pleasure every inch of her. Love every inch of her.

She gasped as he trailed fervent kisses down her soft neck while his hand gently stroked her perfect breasts.

He had to love her. Now.

With a low growl of pure desire, he swept her into his powerful arms and crossed to the bed. He laid her there and stepped back, looking at her with passion-darkened eyes. Anxious to possess her, his fingers fumbled with the brooch.

She laughed softly at his predicament. "I am impatient, too," she whispered huskily.

He froze. "Impatient?"

His ardor died.

He was acting like some kind of lascivious, lustful lout bent only on fulfilling his own base desires with no thoughts to the consequences. He had forgotten the respect due his host, and her, and what was expected of an honorable knight.

He sat on the end of the bed and ran his hands through his shoulder-length locks.

"What is it?" she asked, raising herself on her elbow to regard him with concern.

"You were right. I was impatient," he replied, glancing at her, disgusted with himself. "I am not normally so."

Flushing, she scrambled off the bed. "I am not like Lisid," she said firmly.

He rose to face her, his countenance contrite. "I am sure of that. It is myself I question, my own haste I condemn. The only excuse I can make is that I have never felt this way before, for any woman."

"I have never felt this way before, either," she confessed.

"Never?"

"Not ever," she confirmed, and his heart swelled with hope and happiness.

He gently took her by the shoulders, regarding her steadily. "I do not do such things lightly, Seona. I never have. Do you understand me?"

"I am glad to hear it."

"I am by nature a cautious man," he continued. "You hardly know me. I hardly know you. I think we must be less...impetuous."

Even as she nodded in agreement, Seona blushed at her own lust and lack of control. Her feelings seemed so overwhelming and powerful, it was as if her emotions and her body had undergone a great and amazing metamorphosis.

If he had not stopped, she would have willingly— and wrongly—made love to him.

He was right to question such strong feelings and where they might lead, yet his words disappointed her nonetheless.

Something of her dismay must have shown on her face, for he gathered her in his arms and pressed a kiss on her forehead.

"What if I want to be impetuous?" she whispered, again filled with a desperate need to be with him. "I would leave here with you tonight, if you asked me to."

"You would?"

"Yes."

He sighed wearily. "I have never had a more tempting proposal."

She looked up at him with pleading eyes. "I want to go away with you. I would go anywhere with you, gladly."

His hands clasped loosely about her waist, he leaned back a little to search her face. "That would destroy any possibility of a trade agreement between our fathers."

"Yes, it would," she replied, stiffening.

"Seona, I want to be with you, too, but I think we must be certain that what we feel is true, not fleeting. We must not let our hearts rule our heads."

She could not deny that he was speaking wisely. She, too, should wish to be sure of his feelings for her, given her parents' disastrous history. "Very well."

He sighed raggedly. "I begin to understand my foster brother a little better."

She gave him a puzzled look.

"Dylan is forever falling in and out of love. I have never understood why he would torture himself so. I begin to see that when it comes to love, one has little choice."

"Griffydd?"

"Yes?"

"Are you saying…you love me?" she asked in a small voice, scarcely daring to believe it was possible.

He nodded solemnly. "If what I feel for you is not love, I have no name to put to it."

"I love you, too," she murmured.

She reached up and kissed him, but only lightly brushing her lips across his. More, and she would demand to stay the night with him.

That was a shameful urge which she should regret.

But she did not.

He groaned softly. "You had better leave me, for I fear all my notions of honor and duty are wavering with you in my arms."

"Mine, too," she admitted, reluctantly leaving his warm embrace.

Griffydd watched her go to the door, astonished at how bereft he felt. He was so tempted to call her back, only the knowledge that she deserved to be treated like a virtuous lady worthy of the utmost respect prevented him from doing so.

She paused on the threshold and glanced back at him.

"Perhaps we should hide these feelings from others," she proposed, "for if my father guessed, he might try to take advantage of you when discussing the trade pact."

"You are a very shrewd and wonderful woman, Seona."

"And you are the most honorable man I have ever met, Griffydd DeLanyea."

Then she grinned merrily, a sparkle of devilment in her big eyes. "And you've got the best knees, too."

Griffydd's low, husky chuckle followed her out into the moonlight, where she danced her way to her quarters, too happy in his love to simply walk.

Chapter Eleven

"I could not do it for less than half!" Diarmad thundered, glaring at Griffydd as the two men sat in his hall toward the noon the next day.

Griffydd regarded his host dispassionately. "One half of the profit seems excessive," he answered calmly.

Diarmad scowled as he reached for his drinking horn, complaining under his breath about men who knew nothing of the dangers of the sea.

Griffydd ignored the man's theatrics, reflecting that his father had been right about Diarmad's bluster and protestations. Griffydd had partaken of negotiations before, and some with men of the same sort as Diarmad, but none had been so extreme in their behavior.

It had taken all morning for Griffydd to finally get Diarmad to discuss actual terms for the transport of his father's goods. The chieftain had wasted considerable time grumbling about the type of goods, claiming he preferred silver jewelry to bullion or even coin, and declaring that wool was too light a cargo, unless it got wet. Then it got too heavy, so how could a man judge the ballast?

If Griffydd had been in any particular hurry to leave Dunloch, he would have pressed the man to get to the important points of the pact with more persistence; as it was, he allowed Diarmad to complain as much as he liked.

Nevertheless, he was now starting to wonder if Diarmad's complaints had less to do with the desire to make a good bargain than a reconsideration of the whole notion of a trade pact with Baron DeLanyea.

Perhaps the arrival of a jarl had not been a coincidence, but was intended to force Diarmad to reconsider the proposed pact.

Griffydd had no evidence one way or the other. Indeed, he had yet to meet the other important visitor to Dunloch. He had noted the Norseman's absence from the hall that morning to break the fast. As a visitor, the jarl should have accepted the hospitality of his host, and that meant eating with him.

Perhaps the Norseman's nonattendance meant that this visit was nothing out of the ordinary and its purpose as Seona had said, a collection of the tribute due Haakon. If so, the jarl could simply be sleeping off the effects of too much wine and ale.

"I've got to pay for the food for the men and the sails and lines. And then there's the risk," Diarmad said.

"Your ships will make voyages with or without my father's goods aboard, so I see no reason he should be penalized for risk."

"But perhaps they would not sail to those places without his silver and wool."

"Or perhaps they might. And it will not be your goods that will be lost, should the ship go down."

"It will be my men and my ship!" Diarmad cried, slamming his fist down on the table so that his drinking horn rattled.

"Yes," Griffydd agreed, ignoring the man's gesture, "but otherwise, it would be your goods, as well as your men and your ship."

Diarmad threw himself back in his heavy chair and scowled at the Welshman. "You're a coldhearted fellow!" he grumbled.

Griffydd didn't respond. Coldhearted? He might have agreed before he came to Dunloch. Now he knew otherwise, or thoughts of Seona, such as where she was and what she might be doing, wouldn't be distracting him. Nor would his sleep have been filled with restless dreams of Seona in his arms, fully his wife.

"A third, then!" Diarmad offered grumpily.

"A third, when it will be my father's men who load and unload the ships? Your men will have no extra work there."

"Just the sailing of the vessel, which *I* have built!"

"Which they would be doing anyway. However," Griffydd said as he eyed his opponent, "my father will agree to let you select the ports, so that your men will have no especial peril there. He also trusts to your superior knowledge of where the goods will fetch the best price."

"Huh," Diarmad snorted before taking another gulp of the strong ale.

The sound told Griffydd the idea was not without merit in the man's sight. "Of course, should the risk still trouble you, there are always men from the Lowlands who might be willing—"

"Do you call those things they use *ships?*" Diarmad demanded. "They're like tubs wallowing in a pond."

"Oh?" Griffydd replied. "Have you not seen their new design? The way the rudder is in the stern? They tell us it makes for better steering."

Diarmad's eyes narrowed. "You've seen one?"

"My father has."

"And your father's been talking to the commander of one of them, eh?"

"He met one of the captains in London this past autumn. He was quite impressed with the ship, and the captain, too."

"Come!" Diarmad suddenly ordered, jumping to his feet.

Griffydd scrambled after the chieftain as he marched out of the hall. Outside, Diarmad headed toward the beach and the buildings on the shore.

A light drizzle fell from a gray sky and mist shrouded the tops of the craggy hills surrounding Dunloch. Far from being unpleasant, it almost felt as if he were back in Wales, Griffydd reflected.

That thought pleased him, for perhaps Seona would not miss her homeland very much if she came to live in Wales.

As Griffydd continued to follow Diarmad like a

small boat being towed behind a larger vessel, his gaze searched the village on the chance he would see Seona.

He did not, and soon they reached a long building on the shore near a narrow wooden pier. Outside the building, wood, both logs and planks, was piled. In a smaller adjacent building lit by a glowing fire, some men, obviously smiths, were making what looked like nails. Sparks filled the air around them and made hissing sounds when they met the rain, yet the men seemed oblivious to everything but their work. From inside the larger building came the sound of hammering and men talking.

Diarmad went to the end of this building and disappeared around the corner. Griffydd followed him and found himself in a boat shed, staring at what would surely be one of the finest longships he had ever seen, with one important difference.

Instead of being a separate piece over the right side of the vessel, the steering board was in the stern. It was like the Lowlanders' ship his father had described wedded to the Norsemen's superior, sleek design.

"It is a birlinn and a lovely ship it will be," Diarmad boasted, glancing at Griffydd. "Swift as the wind."

All the men working fell silent and moved away when they realized they had visitors in their midst, leaving Griffydd a clear path to walk around the vessel. He did so, admiring the ship for the thing of beauty it was.

"*This* is what I would use to transport your father's goods," Diarmad announced. "They will be to market and back before he has hardly missed them. Surely that is worth a third of the profit.''

"This does look like a fine ship," Griffydd said, resisting the urge to run his hand along the overlapping planks of the hull.

Diarmad came around Griffydd to face him and gestured at what was clearly his pride and joy. "Is that all you can say, DeLanyea? This will be the finest vessel on the ocean!"

"So it may be," Griffydd conceded. "But that is of less concern to my father than the amount of profit you wish to keep."

Some of the shipbuilders began to mutter, no doubt believing that Griffydd was insulting their handiwork.

Especially the grizzled old man who looked to be in charge. His stern gaze was enough to remind Griffydd that even if their task was to build ships, these men were descended from Vikings, too. It was easy to believe the old man had been a fierce berserker in his youth and would gladly throw an ax in the Welshman's chest for even an implied insult.

Griffydd stepped back and said with obvious admiration, "I have seen no ship to compare with it, though. Tell me, what does your Norse friend think?"

A wary look passed over Diarmad's face before a thundering voice answered the question.

"Haakon will want to see it," a man announced from the entrance.

Griffydd turned to see a large, brawny, blond warrior standing there, a smile slashing his rugged face. He was well dressed in the Norse fashion, with a mulberry-colored silk tunic, embossed belt with a battle ax stuck through it, silver torque and armbands, brown woolen breeches and his booted feet topped with ermin-wrapped leggings.

The fellow strode into the boat shed as if he owned it and ran an appreciative gaze over the vessel.

He said nothing to Griffydd or Diarmad before speaking in Norse to the shipbuilders. Judging by his tone and their respectful and pleased reaction, he was complimenting them and their handiwork.

Finally Diarmad moved. "Olaf," he said to the Norseman, "this is my other guest, Sir Griffydd DeLanyea."

The Norseman glanced over his shoulder and gave Griffydd a dismissive glance. "I thought as much."

"Sir Griffydd, this is Olaf Haraldson, jarl and cousin to King Haakon of Norway."

"I thought as much," Griffydd replied coolly.

The Norseman stopped looking at the ship to turn his surprised visage toward Griffydd. Then he laughed, the sound echoing through the building.

Griffydd did not so much as smile.

Diarmad looked uneasily from one man to the other. "I think we have taken these men from their work long enough," he said after a moment.

"You are interested in ships?" the Norseman asked, again ignoring the chieftain.

"When they are necessary," Griffydd replied.

"A good ship is better than a woman," Olaf remarked, gazing thoughtfully at the incomplete vessel. "Pliant and obedient."

"Fine things in a ship, perhaps," Griffydd observed. "And horses," he continued, glancing sharply at Diarmad. "If you would prefer a thing made of wood to a woman of flesh and blood and spirit, so be it," he finished nonchalantly.

Olaf threw back his head and roared with laughter. "You have me there, Welshman!" he cried jovially. "What is a ship to a willing and beautiful woman, eh? Perhaps, DeLanyea, you would care to know what it is like to sail aboard a really fine ship?" He cocked his head and ran a measuring gaze over Griffydd. "Would you come out with us on my ship today?"

The last thing Griffydd wanted to do was go sailing with a boastful, loud Norseman.

"Or has haggling with Diarmad exhausted you?"

Although the Norseman smiled, there was a challenge in his ice blue eyes.

Griffydd was reminded of the last time he had thought he saw a challenge in a man's eyes, when he had chosen the fighting stallion. He had not been seriously injured then—but what would be the danger of being alone at sea surrounded by a well-trained crew of Norsemen?

He was Sir Griffydd DeLanyea, son of a rich and powerful baron, surely too valuable a person to be murdered, especially when he was also the welcome guest of Diarmad MacMurdoch.

He would not have any man think him a coward, most certainly not an uncouth Norseman or Seona's father.

"I will be most pleased to sail with you."

Later that day, Seona stared unseeing at the small pot of bog myrtle on the ground in front of her. As she sat in silent contemplation, the damp, earthy scent filled her nostrils, and a small fire burning in the open hearth sent spirals of wood smoke curling upward. Another pot half-full of water hung suspended over the fire.

Her mind was far away from her work, thinking of Griffydd and imagining a future she had scarcely dared to dream of before, as the cherished wife of a fine and wonderful man.

If he loved her, would he not seek her hand in marriage?

She smiled secretively, thinking of his need to be cautious. That was only wise, yet she knew in her heart that her feelings for him would never diminish, never change. He was everything she had ever hoped for in a husband, and more.

Once married to him, happy and free at last, she would do everything in her power to make a good household for him.

Then she thought of the children they would have together. Pure, radiant joy filled her as she contemplated that—and then burning desire as she imagined the creation of their babies.

"Well, Seona," Lisid said, entering the dyeing shed, carrying Beitiris and leading Fionn by the hand. "You are here."

Her arrival, although expected, nevertheless made Seona start and flush guiltily because of her recent imaginings. "Where else would I be?"

Lisid didn't deign to respond as she settled Beitiris in a cradle kept there.

Fionn came to stand in front of Seona.

"Where's Griffydd?" he asked plaintively. "I want to see him."

"I don't know," she answered honestly.

"I want to see his horse, too. When can he tell me another story?"

Lisid looked with annoyance at her son, then Seona. "If Fionn had been put to bed earlier," she charged, "he would not be so peevish."

It was on the tip of Seona's tongue to ask Lisid if a similar thing would have made *her* less peevish.

"Sir Griffydd is probably with the chieftain," she explained to Fionn. "They have many things to talk about, but perhaps Sir Griffydd will be able to visit with you again later."

Lisid's eyes gleamed with the superiority of someone who knows something of which others are ignorant. "*I* saw him at the Norseman's ship. Your father was there, too."

Fionn grabbed Seona's hand and started to tug. "Then let's go see him!"

While wondering what the men would be doing there, Seona gently disengaged the boy's grasping hand. "Perhaps later, Fionn. Now be a good boy and let us be about our work."

"Yes, let us be about our work," Lisid repeated in a slightly mocking tone as she eyed first the amount of water Seona had already poured into the pot over the open hearth, then the bog myrtle that would be added later. "Men may play, but women must work," she finished in a grim tone.

Fionn, apparently sensing the futility of persistence, reluctantly went to the corner near the cradle and played with some sticks, diligently constructing a miniature fortress.

Seona reached up to the rafters and pulled down some dried herbs. She broke them into small pieces over another pot.

"I wonder what they were doing at Olaf's ship?" she mused more to herself than Lisid.

"Olaf wanted to show him how well it sails," Lisid replied, taking the small pot of myrtle and sprinkling some in the water. "They were putting out to sea. I need more water."

"Is my father to sail with them, too?" Seona asked as she filled a pot from the bucket, by her tone implying the answer was totally insignificant.

In reality, nothing to do with her father, a Norse jarl and their Welsh-Norman guest could be insignificant.

"I think not. I'm certain DeLanyea will be impressed with the ship," Lisid continued, as proud as if she had designed and built Olaf's vessel herself.

"Yes, I suppose he will," Seona said with a shrug of her shoulders. "I wonder how long they will be out."

"I think only a short time." Lisid straightened. "What does it matter to you?"

"I was concerned about the evening meal," Seona replied, not untruthfully. "I wouldn't want to serve our guests cold meat."

"I should think they will return before it gets dark, don't you?" Lisid said with a smugly mocking smile.

Despite her cherished hope that she would not have to endure Lisid for much longer, Seona had had all she could bear of the woman's manner for the moment. "How do *you* come to know these things?" she asked pointedly.

"I was buying some fish. I have as much right to be on the waterfront as anybody," Lisid replied defensively. "I wasn't eavesdropping."

"I have to get more water," Seona mumbled, picking up the bucket and heading outside.

As she went toward the stream leading to the harbor, she watched the fine longship heading past the broch and out to sea.

Catching the scent of rain, she looked to the north, where high, gray clouds massed in the distance.

Griffydd couldn't help admiring Olaf Haraldson's fine vessel as it sped through the choppy waves of the ocean outside the harbor of Dunloch. Once past the broch, the crew had raised the sail, which caught the stiff breeze, billowing out like the chest of an arrogant Viking.

Now the men lounged against the side of the ship, talking in hushed voices and drinking their ever-present ale.

Despite his confidence in Olaf and his crew when it came to sailing their ship, their apparent easeful manner, and his knowledge that as the son of Baron DeLanyea he was an important man, Griffydd kept a wary eye on the Norsemen. An unforeseen "accident" was not impossible and, he thought as he cast an uneasy eye at the gray clouds to the north, a storm could come up with surprising swiftness, taking them all unawares.

Olaf, too, glanced northward as he came to stand beside Griffydd in the stern, the steersman on the opposite side.

"The weather should hold for some time yet," he said to no one in particular.

"This is a marvelous ship," the Welshman said, not hiding his admiration, or his confidence that he was safe here.

"Yes," Olaf said, and Griffydd waited for the inevitable boast, which did not come.

He eyed the Norseman quizzically. "It is yours?"

"My cousin's."

"Ah. That would be King Haakon?"

The Norseman nodded. "He is like an older brother to me, too," he declared. "I have been in his household since my father died when I was a boy." Olaf gave Griffydd a shrewd glance. "I have heard of your father, the Baron DeLanyea, with his one eye."

"Indeed?"

"Yes. We have something in common, I think. It is not easy being in the household of powerful men."

Griffydd wasn't sure what Olaf was getting at, so he merely nodded.

"And you are part Norman, so a descendent of Norsemen, too."

Again Griffydd nodded, reflecting that Olaf seemed in an oddly meditative mood, which filled him with more suspicion than confidence. "My mother is a Norman, my father half Welsh, half Norman."

Olaf gave him another sidelong glance. "So is your family's loyalty to the Welsh, or the Normans?"

Griffydd kept his gaze focused on the receding

shore. "I have come to Dunloch for a trade agreement."

"I think Diarmad's only loyalty is to profit."

The ship rolled and the deck shifted beneath Griffydd's feet, as if he needed a reminder that he was sailing treacherous waters in more ways than one. "You do not approve of his trade practices?"

Olaf laughed. "Trade is not for jarls to think about. It is the allies Diarmad seeks that draws our notice."

"Obviously you think this trade pact implies an important alliance with my father."

Olaf grinned. "Wouldn't you, if you were in my boots?"

"At present, my father is only interested in using Diarmad's ships," he explained truthfully. "Of course, he does expect that the agreement will also insure that Diarmad will not attack our lands. If Diarmad thinks it means more, he is mistaken."

"Diarmad speaks only of trade, as you do," Olaf admitted. "But you must understand that we have to be watchful of our underlings. Any other form of alliance will be considered an act of betrayal by Haakon and he will retaliate."

The words were calmly spoken, but Griffydd heard the underlying menace. He was glad that he and Seona had agreed to keep their feelings for each other a secret for the time being, no matter how much he disliked anything that even hinted at subterfuge. As he had realized, his marriage to Seona might have other consequences.

He should speak to his father and seek his advice before asking for Seona's hand in marriage. The baron was a diplomatic man with many noble friends. He would surely know how best to proceed in a way that would prevent serious complications.

Nevertheless, anger began to smolder within Griffydd. He deeply resented anyone's interference in his decisions—and did this man think he could threaten him, or his father?

"How kind of you to warn me," Griffydd said after a moment, his even tones betraying nothing of his anger, "and through me, my father, and through my father, King Henry."

Olaf scowled. "Kindness? I warn you as I would an enemy I'm about to attack, DeLanyea, to give them a chance to surrender. Do not seek more of an alliance with Diarmad than the silver you exchange, or my uncle will not think well of it."

"I merely point out that when you threaten my father or me, you should consider to whom we are already allied," Griffydd replied. "I do not think you would want my father for an enemy. As you know, he is a famous warrior with powerful friends. And the DeLanyeas *never* surrender."

Olaf cleared his throat and looked at the toes of his boots before replying. "That is why I would speak with you here, away from Diarmad and his men," he said in a slightly humbler manner. "My uncle would rather not become your father's enemy. I also thought to caution you in your dealings with Diarmad. The man is not to be trusted. He could very well betray us all to the Scots."

"He could, which is why we only talk trade with

him at present, as my father has already made clear to King Henry."

Olaf was clearly taken aback. "He has? He has spoken with your king about doing business with Diarmad MacMurdoch?"

"As he should. Diarmad is not unknown, either. He has too many ships to ignore. My father wanted King Henry to know exactly what he was doing, so there would be no misunderstanding."

"He is a farseeing man," the Norseman said.

"He is that, and we live in turbulent times."

"Aye. You're a man I can respect, DeLanyea," Olaf said, sighing wearily. "These are not easy days for honorable men. We are sent hither and thither like page boys for our overlords."

"I am honored to be entrusted with this responsibility by my father."

Olaf scowled, but Griffydd sensed the Norseman's reaction had little to do with him. "Then you are happier in your task than I."

Given the man's current attitude of camaraderie, Griffydd thought this a good time to attempt to discover more of Olaf's purpose in Dunloch.

Suddenly a shout from a man in the bow made them both look northward, where dark clouds were suddenly rolling rapidly closer.

"Odin's eyes!" Olaf muttered. He cupped his hand around his mouth and bellowed an order.

Instantly the men leaped to their feet. Some began to untie the lines holding the sail and one shinned up the mast. Then he began to lower the sail, while at the same time the remaining men put out their oars. They started to row, without singing.

Slowly, as the wind picked up yet more speed and the waves swelled, the ship turned toward Dunloch.

Then the rain came, heavy droplets whipped by the wind. Combined with the sea spray, Griffydd was drenched in minutes, the taste of salt on his lips.

Dark, angry clouds filled the sky. The ship rocked, tossed like a child's toy as a huge wave caught the stern. The oarsmen, their faces grim with fierce determination, continued to row.

As another wave struck the vessel, Griffydd grabbed for the gunwale and held on, then watched in horror as the ribs of the ship twisted and bent with the force of the churning sea.

"She is built for rougher seas than this," Olaf cried above the wind. "But I will not have her battered for no good reason." He jumped down into the bottom of the ship and reached for an extra oar.

He looked up at Griffydd. "Row!" he commanded above the howling wind.

Chapter Twelve

Wrapped in her cloak, Seona waited in the shadow of the broch, seeking what shelter the remains of the tower provided against the storm that had arisen so suddenly. Her gaze anxiously scanned the sea and the mouth of the harbor. Other men, her father among them, waited near the wharf, also keeping watch for Olaf's longship.

What if it were already gone beneath the waves? What if Griffydd was drowned?

The anguish was so great, she would not allow herself to think that again.

He was on one of the finest vessels she had ever seen. Olaf was a skilled seaman, as would be all his crew. They would have spotted the storm coming and turned back.

Surely they would not have sailed out of sight of land, and so if…if the worst happened, those thrown into the sea could swim to shore.

Unless Olaf had felt the need to impress a Welshman and gone too far out.

And those trying to swim to the shore could have their brains dashed out upon the rocks.

She moaned softly, black despair momentarily overwhelming her. Covering her face with her hands, she prayed to God, pleading with Him to spare Griffydd's life.

A shout made her drop her hands and peer out into the rain.

The Norse longship appeared at the entrance of the harbor, oars churning.

Anxiously she searched the vessel. Where was Griffydd? She could not see anyone standing in the stern.

Could he have gotten swept over the side?

Gathering up her sodden skirt and cloak, she ran along the top of the bluff, not taking her eyes from the ship, counting the crew—and then she saw him, seated in the stern, sharing an oar with Olaf.

"Thank God!" she cried, looking to the clouded heavens as relief and gratitude filled her.

Quickening her pace, she hurried through the village toward the waterfront. Once there, she stayed behind the crowd of men milling about despite the rain. With happy relief, she watched the crew ship their oars and the vessel glide to the wharf.

She had no business there. Nevertheless, she wanted to be near Griffydd. Needed to be near him.

She maneuvered her way closer to the ship.

"Hail, Olaf!" her father cried out, his words carried on the wind. "We feared for you!"

Olaf and Griffydd rose together, their soaking hair and garments clinging to their bodies.

"How could you doubt my ship?" Olaf replied indignantly, shaking his wet hair out of his eyes.

Then he grinned and nodded at the equally sodden Griffydd. "I had to convince him of the superiority of our vessels."

"I would say you have succeeded," Griffydd replied laconically.

Seona smiled with more relief at their friendly banter. Then she caught Griffydd's eye and smiled.

He did not smile back, yet there came a look to his eyes that told her he had seen her, and was glad.

"I tell you, I have aged a year," Diarmad declared as Olaf and Griffydd joined him on the wharf, where he handed them thick cloaks. "It is not a good thing to frighten a man of my years."

"I thought the only thing you feared was losing money," Olaf replied, throwing the cloak over his soaking shoulders.

"That, too," Diarmad agreed. "Both of you must join me in the hall. I have a good fire and the best food, and plenty of mulled wine to take off the chill."

Olaf nodded and went to follow Diarmad, but Griffydd held back. "I would prefer to get into dry clothes first."

Seona thought of the large, chilly interior of the guest quarters.

With joy-lightened feet, she once again picked up her damp skirts and hurried away.

He had not felt so physically exhausted since his years of training under Fitzroy, Griffydd reflected as he wearily trudged toward the guest quarters. He would be glad of warm, dry clothing—although not so glad as he had been to see Seona smiling at him.

He wondered where she had gone, then decided she must have to help in the hall, preparing the evening meal and the refreshments for Olaf and his equally weary crew.

He entered his longhouse and saw Seona at once, standing beside a lit brazier. The warmth of the fire enveloped him, although even that was not as welcome as the sight of Seona's smiling face.

How easy it was to imagine that she was his wife welcoming him home!

"Seona!" he cried happily—then propriety, and his own notions of honorable behavior, reminded him that they should not be alone together in such intimate circumstances. "Should you not be in the hall? Won't people wonder where you are?"

"I thought you might be cold...."

She hesitated, flushing prettily and lowering her gaze in a demure manner vastly different from Lisid's coy looks.

"So you came to prepare this fire for me?" he said softly. "I am delighted."

He went toward her, tempted to take her in his arms. He would have, had he not been soaking wet.

"You had best get out of those clothes, lest you fall ill," Seona suggested.

"Remember, I don't get sick from being wet. Still," he said wryly, "this is not a comfortable state."

He threw off the cloak and went to his chest, looking for some linen with which to dry, as well as fresh clothes.

"Griffydd, I was so afraid!" Seona whispered. "I thought you might be drowned."

"I confess I envisioned such a fate myself, especially when I realized the ship's ribs were bending like willow branches and weren't nailed to the vessel."

"They are tied with spruce roots," she told him. "It lets the hull twist, so it will not break from the force of the waves."

"Whether Olaf intended it or not, I have had a most impressive lesson in the quality of Norse ships."

Seona smiled again. "While I am glad it was not a fatal one."

He tossed some dry clothes onto the bed, then peeled off his tunic. He found a square of linen and, sitting on a stool, started to rub his hair. "Olaf also wanted to warn me about making an alliance with your father."

"Warn you?"

"Yes." Griffydd didn't keep the sarcasm from his

voice as he continued. "He very kindly thought I should realize that any alliance my family makes with your father could have serious ramifications. He also seems to think your father might make a compact with the Scots."

Seona shook her head at that. "No, not them. He thinks they will never amount to much, that they are all fools who would rather argue among themselves over who shall be their king than seek prosperity." She frowned, puzzled. "You and Olaf seemed very friendly when you landed."

"We understand each other, that's all. I would rather have someone tell me to my face what he thinks. I hate subterfuge."

"I do not like it, either," she replied.

He threw aside the linen and rose, reaching out to pull her into his arms. He gently kissed her forehead. "Thank you for preparing this welcome for me."

"I should leave you now," Seona said regretfully. "If anyone were to discover me here…"

"It would not be good," he confirmed.

"I have to leave you," she repeated softly, even as she closed her eyes, so happy in his strong embrace.

"I know. I agree."

Despite his words, he began to kiss her, soft, tender kisses that held the promise of barely suppressed passion.

A passion that, unlike him, she did not want to subdue. Instead, she eagerly sought his mouth.

With a low moan of feverish desire, he responded.

Their kiss deepened as more of their passionate desire blossomed forth.

Then all too soon, if reluctantly, he pulled away. "You are indeed a temptress."

She shook her head. "You are the tempting one, kissing me like that."

He smiled wryly, his eyes merry. "I believe you are right. It must be because I am so exhausted that I am so forgetful of propriety."

Then another look came to his face. "I think you had best leave me. I have only so much strength left and it is waning fast."

"Yes, I must go," she agreed reluctantly as she pulled away and went to the door.

When she heard him yawn, she glanced back over her shoulder to see Griffydd lying on the bed, one arm carelessly thrown over his face.

"God's wounds, I've never been so tired in my life," he muttered.

Before she could bid him farewell, she realized he was asleep.

Later that evening, dressed in the *brat* and *chroich,* a drinking horn loose in his hand, Griffydd sat in Diarmad's hall and gravely contemplated the men around him. He would far rather contemplate Seona, but she was not in the hall at the moment.

She had gone to fetch more ale. Olaf Haraldson and his men seemed to have a limitless capacity for the beverage—so much so, Griffydd had long ago lost count of the number of horns they had consumed.

The wonder of it was that Olaf was still capable of coherent talk. Griffydd would have preferred the boisterous, loudmouthed fellow to have passed out long ago, for Olaf's booming voice dominated all others in the hall. A man could scarcely think, let alone discuss anything of note while he held forth.

Not that Griffydd was anxious to discuss anything of note in Olaf's presence. Diarmad was obviously of the same mind, for the talk had been all inconsequential and meaningless banter.

Nor was Griffydd the only one apparently disturbed by Olaf's presence. Naoghas looked even more glum than usual, and several others matched his sullenness. The one named Eodan watched Diarmad and Olaf like a man seeking a calm bay before a storm and the religious fellow, Iosag, crossed himself whenever the Norseman came near him, despite the large crucifix Olaf wore.

Griffydd didn't blame Iosag. He could more easily believe that the silver, bejeweled cross was merely another bit of finery to the Norseman.

Griffydd glanced again at Olaf, seated to their host's right, the side of most prestige. He did not fault Diarmad for that; by rights, a jarl related to a king outranked a Norman knight.

As Olaf and Diarmad began to argue about the merits of the stern steering board versus having the device over the right side of the vessel, Seona walked into the hall carrying a jug of ale. As always, she was plainly dressed in a loose-fitting, belted woolen gown, today the color of sand. Her long hair was bound back in a single braid, so he could easily see her fascinating face.

He fought the urge to stare at her as she moved along the tables, the light adding compelling angles and shadows to her elfin face.

He could watch her all night.

Despite his resolve not to betray any special feelings for her, he could not help smiling a little when she glanced at him. It took a man watching closely to notice that her lips twitched in a similar small smile of response, yet for that brief moment, it was as if they were alone.

Olaf rose, swaying as if he were on the deck of his ship in rough weather. It seemed that the amount of ale he had imbibed had finally penetrated his brain.

"Your ale is good, Diarmad, yet does not linger," he announced with a wide grin and a slight bow before making his way down the hall.

He staggered a little as he passed Seona without acknowledging her.

Griffydd glared at Olaf as he went outside. He was not at all pleased to see Seona so rudely treated by anyone, even if the fellow was a jarl, and drunk to boot.

Seona caught his eye and must have realized how angered he was by the man's impolite treatment, for she gave a little shake of her head. Obviously she did not want him to say anything about this rudeness. As much as Griffydd hated remaining silent, she was right. It was not his place, as a guest, to chastise anyone for not according Seona the respect she merited by rank alone, if nothing else.

But when she was his wife, he silently vowed, he would see she was always treated with the respect she so richly deserved.

"A third is not too much," Diarmad suddenly announced, eyeing Griffydd while he ripped off a piece of the salted herring in front of him.

Obviously, Diarmad had decided to negotiate when he thought his potential trading partner half-drunk.

Unfortunately for Diarmad, Griffydd had been dumping his ale on the floor under the table. It wasn't being absorbed by the packed earth immediately, but Griffydd was far less concerned about sticky boots than he was about keeping his wits about him.

"A tenth is what my father considered fair," Griffydd replied, just as easily returning to their negotiations, which had been so abruptly interrupted that morning.

"What?" Diarmad cried, nearly choking. He spit out the piece of fish. "A tenth!"

"Alas, I fear your ale is making me light-headed," Griffydd replied evenly. "I beg leave to wait until tomorrow to discuss this, when we can speak in private."

"I think we could decide tonight," Diarmad declared.

"I do not," Griffydd said, and even Diarmad heard the tone of finality.

"Aye, perhaps you're right," he muttered, stroking his beard. "But a tenth," he continued in a low grumble. "That's an insult!"

Diarmad did seem truly upset by the initial amount, so Griffydd felt it appropriate to indicate that this was merely a preliminary figure.

"On the contrary, I think it a fine...starting point," Griffydd replied.

Out of the corner of his eye, Griffydd noticed Olaf return.

Diarmad relaxed slightly, then also glanced at Olaf. "As you say, perhaps this is not the time for such important discussions."

The Norseman made his way around the table, sighing robustly as he sat heavily. Surely the man would want to retire soon and leave them in some peace.

Then Lisid entered the hall, carrying more flat bread. As if by some secret signal, all the men in the hall looked at her, Griffydd included.

She was certainly what most men would consider beautiful, as their constant attention proved, he reflected. Tonight she was very finely dressed in a light woolen gown of cornflower blue covered by an overtunic of yellow. A necklace of polished stones set in silver was about her neck, and a similar bracelet graced her wrist. She used cosmetics, for her eyes were circled with a dark substance, and he suspected the ruby tint of her lips was not natural.

Out of the corner of his eye, Griffydd caught the brief frown that crossed Diarmad's face when he saw her, his gaze on the necklace.

It did not take much effort to guess where Lisid had gotten that, and he vaguely wondered what excuse she had made to her husband.

Griffydd dispassionately watched Lisid approach their table and slowly set the bread in front of Olaf. She gave the Norseman a coy smile.

"Where are your children?" Griffydd asked.

She glanced at him as if he were an annoying insect. "With one of the other women," she replied pertly.

Then, after again smiling at Olaf, she sauntered away.

Vaguely disgusted with her obvious flirtation, Griffydd looked for Seona and saw her standing near Naoghas, who was watching his wife, a scowl darkening his face.

He was reminded of the fighting stallions and the mare used to inspire them to attack each other.

By now, Seona had moved closer to the high table, refilling drinking horns. At last she came to Griffydd, and he held out his empty drinking horn.

She gave him a curious glance, probably wondering how drunk he was, for she had refilled it many times. He risked a wink and a quick look at the floor, and was rewarded by the smile in her eyes.

Unfortunately—but wisely—she did not linger. She moved on to her father, then Olaf.

"I will say this for you, Diarmad," Olaf declared gruffly, and very loudly. "You have the most beautiful woman in this hall I have ever beheld."

Diarmad's expression was both surprised and scornful. "I would never call Seona a beauty."

Griffydd stiffened slightly and glanced at Seona, who couldn't have avoided hearing the conversation if her ears were filled with beeswax. Nevertheless, the only sign she gave that she had heard herself disparaged was a deepening flush on her cheeks.

Griffydd wanted to bellow at both Diarmad and Olaf for upsetting her. He would have enjoyed knocking their thick heads together, too.

Olaf looked as if he thought Diarmad must have suddenly gone mad. "I was speaking of Lisid. She is as lovely as a goddess!"

It was all Griffydd could do to keep silent. Could they not see that there was nothing beyond a pretty face and preening vanity to Lisid? There was no fierce, independent intelligence burning in her eyes and no genuine passion in her cold kiss, which had been as unwelcome as Seona's was desired. Lisid was a lovely bauble whose appeal he could comprehend, if not share, while Seona was a living, breathing, spirited woman who could make a man's life complete.

God's wounds, he wanted to take Seona away from here!

Unfortunately, as a guest in Diarmad's hall, he

could only sit and wait for another opportunity to catch Seona's eye, to try to let her know that they were as wrong as men could be.

"Now there's a fellow enjoying what he sees," the Norseman declared with a throaty chuckle, nodding at Naoghas as Lisid set more food before her husband. "Look at the way he's staring at her breasts when she bends over. Like a wolf scenting fresh meat."

"That fellow's her husband," Diarmad said just loud enough for those closest to him to hear.

"By Thor's hammer, he is a fortunate fellow."

"He is also a jealous fellow," Griffydd noted, "so perhaps you should keep your compliments to yourself."

"What, can I not declare the man has a lovely wife?" the Norseman demanded incredulously. Then he called to Naoghas. "You have a wife as beautiful as Freya! I drink to your good fortune!"

With that, he put the drinking horn to his lips and took a massive gulp of the ale. Some of the drink spilled from the sides and ran down his beard.

Griffydd tried not to look disgusted as he scanned the hall. He couldn't see Seona now, but Lisid was certainly present, attempting to look modestly shocked by Olaf's words, yet not able to hide her vain pride.

Naoghas shot a glance at his preening wife, and after a long moment, raised his mug in a salute. Around him, others followed suit, albeit with sidelong glances at their companion and his wife before drinking.

"I need more ale!" Olaf cried, setting down his horn with a bang. "What lovely wench will satisfy my craving?" He leered at Lisid, his meaning all too obvious.

She made as if to move, until Naoghas, clearly angered, muttered something and she hesitated, her lips pouting petulantly.

Griffydd's hand drifted toward his weapon, anticipating a fight. Was the Norseman a simpleton, that he didn't see where his foolish speech was heading?

Suddenly a woman's voice called out with clarion clearness from the entry. "More ale? Of course! More ale for the king's well-mannered cousin!"

Now it was Olaf's turn to scowl as Seona came sauntering forth, a pitcher balanced on her slender hip and on her face a smile that held no mirth.

Griffydd, like every man in the hall, stared at her, wondering what she intended to do. That she was going to do *something* he didn't doubt.

"I don't want you to satisfy any needs of mine," Olaf grumbled thickly.

"Good," she retorted, coming to stand before the high table.

"Seona!" her father warned.

She ignored Diarmad and didn't look at Griffydd, all her attention focused on Olaf. "Alas, cousin of King Haakon, I fear that as my father's daughter, I must see that you get enough food for your belly and all the ale you crave, no matter how rude you are. Now if you will allow me, my lord,'' she said, holding out the pitcher.

The Norseman grudgingly lifted his drinking horn.

Then Seona dumped the entire contents of the pitcher over his head.

Chapter Thirteen

It was all Griffydd could do not to laugh out loud at the spluttering Norseman. A few of the men around him chortled, and others started to mutter appreciatively.

Until Diarmad jumped to his feet.

"You stupid wench!" he snarled at Seona.

Griffydd half rose, even though he had no clear idea what he was going to do or say, save come to her defense.

"Sir Griffydd, please be seated," Seona said gravely, but with a twinkle of defiant pleasure in her large eyes. "Since you have comported yourself with dignity and respect for my father and his household, you have nothing to fear from me."

God's wounds, this is a woman worthy to be a warrior's wife! Griffydd thought appreciatively as he obeyed. Such spirit! Such deserved pride!

Olaf shook his head so that droplets of ale flew about. "By Thor's thunder, Diarmad," he growled, "is this the way you allow your daughter to treat an honored guest?"

"Your pardon, my lord, I fear I am a stupid creature," Seona said with a mocking smile. "I did not realize a man who is so loudly insulting to a woman of my father's hall *was* an honorable guest."

"Seona," Diarmad muttered between clenched teeth. "You have shamed me. Leave this hall!"

"Gladly," she replied with great dignity, setting down the pitcher before turning on her heel and strolling from the hall as if in no great hurry.

His eyes full of admiration, Griffydd watched her go and wondered how long he must wait before he could follow her and praise her for her actions.

Meanwhile, Lisid hurriedly grabbed a cloth from one of the other servants, who had used it to protect her hands from a hot pot. She then rushed forward and handed it to Olaf with a sympathetic smile.

Barely acknowledging her presence, he snatched the cloth and started to wipe his face.

Diarmad's irritated gaze swept over the men before he turned to face Olaf.

"Again, forgive me," he said with a humble bow. "It is to my shame that my daughter has disgraced me so."

"I trust you will make her understand that was not a wise thing to do," Olaf mumbled angrily, glancing sharply at the chieftain.

"Aye, aye, I will, my lord."

"I suggest you waste no time."

Diarmad drew himself up. "It is not for even you

to command me in my own hall,'' he reminded Olaf coldly.

The Norseman rose, an incredulous yet warning expression on his face as he faced Diarmad. They looked like two rams about to butt heads, and tension filled the hall.

"If you will excuse me," Griffydd interrupted calmly, also getting to his feet, "I fear the hour grows late. I believe I should retire." He ran a bland look over the Norseman. "I would get out of those wet clothes, Olaf, if I were you, lest you take a chill."

"Where are you going in such a hurry?" Olaf demanded. "I am the one soaking wet."

"Then you should go and dry off," Griffydd replied. "As you said, the ale does not linger."

"There is no need for you to leave, Sir Griffydd. Please, stay and enjoy the hospitality of my hall," Diarmad said, his words almost a command.

"And while I appreciate your concern for my health," Olaf said, "I have been wetter than this for days at sea. Stay and drink with me. I would hear of your father's journey to the Holy Land."

"Aye, the two of you stay here," Diarmad said placatingly.

Griffydd wanted nothing more than to leave and go to Seona. Unfortunately, if he did that, they might suspect there was something between them, and he was not yet ready to have his feelings known.

Therefore, he had little choice but to sit again.

At Diarmad's next words, however, he felt he had made the wrong choice.

"Excuse me, Olaf, Griffydd," Diarmad said, his

expression returning to one of fierce anger. "I must have words with my daughter."

And then Diarmad strode from the hall.

Her breathing rushed and shallow, Seona stood in her small house at the edge of the village, waiting in the dark. Her father was going to come. She knew it. He had been too angry not to follow and chastise her for what she had done.

As she waited, she imagined how it would be. First, he would berate her, citing yet again her numerous faults and sins. Next he would demand an explanation, to which he would not listen. Then he would punish her.

It was this prospect that made her nervous and wonder if she had been foolhardy, not brave.

Perhaps she had gone too far, emboldened by the knowledge that one man admired her. Respected her. Cared for her.

After all, Olaf had only said what so many men thought.

She wondered what her father would consider a fit punishment. He might order her to apologize to their guest. Or he might command her to keep to her quarters in disgrace—which would mean she would have to risk more trouble if she wanted to see Griffydd.

Perhaps her father might even beat her.

He had never done so before, but this time she had dared to shame him in public. Before, when she had quarreled with him, they had always been alone.

"Seona!"

Even though she had been expecting her father's

arrival, she started like a frightened rabbit, then willed herself to be as calm as she could, and to remember a finer man's opinion of her.

"Are you here?" Diarmad demanded, peering around the dark building. "Do you think you can hide from me, girl?"

She struck flint and stone, then lit an oil lamp so that he could see her.

Diarmad glared at this insolent female who had insulted the cousin of his king and who was going to unite his clan with the royal house of Norway, no matter what she thought of Olaf.

"I wasn't hiding," she declared with a familiar bravado.

"Then you should be," he snarled, his anger growing with the painful memories that flooded through him, of a red-haired woman who had fought him and enraged him and betrayed him. "How dare you insult our guest in that way? He'll probably sail off tomorrow and return with a fleet to attack us."

"Because I poured some ale on his head?" Seona asked skeptically, wrapping her slender arms about herself.

Diarmad marched closer to her, then reached out and hauled her close. "Listen to me, girl! He's a powerful man, and you've done a stupid thing!"

She twisted away. "Maybe I did," she conceded. "But have you no pride?"

"Who are you to question me, or my pride?" her father snarled. "Or to shame me in my hall? What does it matter if he stared at Lisid and made a few remarks? What you did was worse. God's teeth, you're like your mother!''

''Whose head did she dump ale on?'' Seona inquired, her eyes flashing with anger. ''Yours?''

''If she did, it was after we were wed, not before!''

Seona's eyes narrowed. ''What do you mean?''

''You stupid wench, you're about to be given a great honor, one you don't deserve! You are betrothed to Olaf Haraldson!''

At his words, ringing of truth, a stone seemed to plummet into her stomach. She could scarcely breathe, or think. ''Olaf Haraldson? I am to marry him?''

''I could hardly believe our good fortune myself, but it's true.''

This was a nightmare, a hideous dream. ''You said I was to please Griffydd DeLanyea,'' she reminded him. ''Do you no longer care about a pact with his father, so now you will offer me to Olaf like an old *brat* you no longer want?''

''Haakon himself proposed the match, so I could not refuse. Not would I. Olaf is a cousin of the king,'' he repeated. He fastened his cold, unfeeling gaze upon her. ''Finally you are going to do something truly useful. As for the trade pact, this betrothal proves my loyalty to Haakon, so there is no reason it should not happen.''

Trying not to let her extreme dismay cloud her mind, Seona forced herself to think as he would. ''Has it not occurred to you, Father, that a Welshman, even one with Norman blood, might take your alliance with Olaf as a sign that you are completely loyal to Haakon, and therefore a threat to the Welsh?''

"That is why you will say nothing to anyone about this betrothal until the Welshman has gone. I don't want DeLanyea to think I no longer want his father's trade."

"Oh, no, we cannot have that," Seona said sarcastically.

"You have no right to question me or my decisions, girl!" her father growled. "I do what I think best—and if you can repay me in some small measure for the shame your mother caused me, you should be grateful."

"Grateful!" she cried scornfully, her hands curling into fists. "Why not set me up on an auction block like a slave!" She came closer, her gaze accusing. "You hate me that much, I know. Would that not be simpler?"

"Aye, it would. But you will marry Olaf all the same!"

"I don't care if he's the heir to the throne. I will not marry him!" she declared.

Her father ground his fist into his large palm. "By heaven, if I order you to, you will!"

"But—!"

"But nothing, girl!" her father cried, glaring at her. "You're a chieftain's daughter, so if Haakon's cousin is ordered to wed you by the king's command, we have no choice, either. It is the king's will that prevails. And we've clasped hands—" Diarmad paused, as if he had just remembered that himself. "Thank

God, we've clasped hands,'' he finished with obvious relief.

Now the marriage agreement could only be broken with great shame on the side of the party who did so. Financial reparations would have to be made, too.

Her father would never make any reparations for her, Seona realized as a sense of impending doom washed over her.

"Try to use your wits, Seona," Diarmad said in a more reasonable tone. "If we don't do as Haakon wills, he might attack the village and sell us all for slaves. Is that what you'd like better?"

"Surely he wouldn't—"

"He would," her father replied with a tone of absolute conviction.

Desperation and hopelessness filled her heart. She felt trapped, like a deer being chased by a pack of dogs to the edge of a cliff.

Perhaps if she told him about Griffydd and what seemed to be happening between them... "Father—"

"Seona," he interrupted, and suddenly she saw not the stern, forbidding father of her childhood, or the canny trader, or the harsh taskmaster. She saw a tired, bitter old man. "Seona, this marriage is arranged. It is going to happen, because it must. Haakon wills it, and trust me, it would be the worse for all of us if it does not come to pass. We have no choice in this. Not you. Not Olaf. Not me."

"You honestly think that Haakon would attack us if we broke this betrothal?" she asked, not wanting to believe it.

"He would see it as a betrayal, and fear I am mak-

ing other alliances. He will call me a traitor, and all
our people, too. I have met Haakon, and I know in
my bones he would not hesitate to burn this village
to the ground.''

''How can anything we do frighten a king?''

''Can you not just accept what I say?'' Diarmad
growled. ''You must wed Olaf, or we will all suffer.''

He truly believed that what he said would come to
pass if she did not marry Haakon's cousin.

But didn't she deserve some happiness? Had her
life not been miserable enough?

Had it been miserable enough to see Fionn and
Beitiris and everyone else she cared for in the village
sold into slavery, or even killed? To see the bodies
of her father and his warriors lying on the stony
ground, and Dunloch a burned-out ruin?

She knew what Norsemen were capable of, and she
knew that her father's words had, for once, been truthful and sincere. He feared Haakon's wrath, and so
must she.

She was a chieftain's daughter, and she had a duty
to her people.

''Very well, Father,'' she said, defeated, all her
hopes destroyed, all her dreams turned to dust. ''I will
marry Olaf.'' She raised her eyes and regarded her
father steadily. ''And I agree we should say nothing
to Griffydd DeLanyea.''

She would not be able to bear his disappointment,
too.

Diarmad nodded, and in his beady eyes she thought
she saw a glimmer of respect—now, when it did not
matter. ''This is settled, then,'' he said wearily. ''We

will say nothing to anyone else, in case it makes young DeLanyea loath to conclude the trade agreement. While I care about the villagers, if I can make a profit as well as keep them safe, I'm not fool enough to say no.''

She nodded, knowing that for an undeniable truth, too.

Her father looked at her once more, then went out into the night.

Leaving her alone, with no one to witness her anguish or hear her muffled sobs.

Keeping to the shadows, Griffydd hurried cautiously through the village. He silently cursed his inability to leave the hall any earlier. If only Olaf had departed, he would have, too. Instead, wary of raising any suspicions in the man's mind about his feelings for Seona, he had lingered a little longer, until the strain of wondering what her father might do drove him to excuse himself.

If only he could be certain which of the small longhouses near the broch was hers! He dare not enter the wrong one, nor was he even certain that would be where she had gone. Perhaps she had fled elsewhere to seek solace from a friend, or simply to avoid her father.

The moon was covered by a thin layer of cloud, dimming its already meager light. While that meant he stood less chance of being seen—and he must not be seen entering Seona's quarters, lest it lead to additional trouble for her—it also meant his search was more difficult.

Staying in the shadows of the walls, he made his way closer to the outskirts of the village.

Seona had said she lived alone in a small house on the edge of the village near the ruined tower.

There was one longhouse there, little more than a hut, really, that caught his eye. It looked lonely, away by itself, aloof from the others. Like Seona.

He was about to cross the open space between the buildings when someone came out of the little dwelling.

Diarmad.

That had to be Seona's house, and Diarmad still looked infuriated.

Griffydd ducked back into the shadows. Although he was being cautious for Seona's sake, he couldn't help feeling vaguely disgusted with himself, as if he were some kind of thief. He watched the chieftain march past, toward his hall.

He hoped he was not too late.

Even more anxious than before, Griffydd silently dashed across the open space and ducked under the covering over the door of the small house. Once inside, he found himself standing in a very tidy room with a low roof and few furnishings.

"Seona!" he called out softly, suddenly fearful that this might not be her house, after all.

"Yes?" she replied quietly.

Seona sat on a narrow bed, looking at him through the curtain of her magnificent hair.

He gently pulled her to her feet, then enfolded her in his arms.

"Seona!" he whispered. "My wonderful, brave, foolhardy Seona!"

Her shoulders shook as she wept, evidence that her father must have been brutal to her, in words if not in action.

Griffydd put his knuckle under her chin and raised her tear-streaked, downcast face. "I should have gotten here sooner."

When she still would not meet his gaze, he frowned.

"Your father didn't hurt you, did he?" he charged, fighting to keep any menace from his voice, although if Diarmad had laid a hand on her, he would gladly beat the man until he cried for mercy.

She shook her head as she sighed raggedly. "No."

She wiped her face with the back of her hand and looked at him. Then she made an attempt to smile. "I fear I am not as wise as I should be. I...I shamed our whole village by my hasty act."

"It is Olaf and Lisid who should be ashamed," Griffydd said firmly. "Olaf was acting as if he were in some tavern, not a chieftain's hall. And as for Lisid...well, one day, she will find her beauty has deserted her, and that will be punishment enough for one like her."

Seona nodded. "I suppose."

He held her tenderly, cherishing her.

Loving her.

"We shall soon leave this place, and him," he vowed softly, "and when you are my wife, no one will ever hurt you again. I give you my word, the word of Sir Griffydd DeLanyea." Then he knelt before her like the humble petitioner he felt himself to be. "Seona MacMurdoch, will you accept my offer of marriage?"

Seona stared at the man she loved, her heart breaking. All her life, she had dared to dream, despite everything, that a man might one day love her, yet now, when the seemingly impossible had come to pass, when she herself returned that love, she had to refuse it.

"Seona, what is it?" Griffydd demanded warily when she did not answer right away. "Have I made a mistake? Have I spoken too hastily?"

She tried to muster the strength to tell him that he had and that they could not be married. She had to tell him about the betrothal that had been arranged and sealed without her knowledge or consent. She must reveal that she had to go through with this marriage to a man she abhorred, or her whole village might suffer. She had to let him know that she could not put her personal happiness, or his, before the good of so many others, especially the children. They did not deserve slavery or death by the sword because *she* was in love. She had a duty to her people and she could not shirk it, or there would be terrible consequences.

Yet the words that would ruin her chance of happiness would not come. She could not bring herself to destroy their love.

"Nothing would make me happier than to be your wife," she confessed instead.

His smile was so glorious it pained her anew.

"It will not be long before we can be married, I

promise, Seona!'' he cried happily, jumping to his feet. ''I will take you away from here and everyone who doesn't value you.'' He grew serious. ''First, though, I must return home.''

He hurried to explain. ''It is not that I seek a delay. I would marry you this instant, if I could. But you must know, my love, that any marriage a chieftain's daughter and a baron's son makes will set people to pondering alliances and loyalties. I thought I would ask my father, who is very wise in these matters, how best to insure that people understand I am not interested in Seona MacMurdoch because she is a chieftain's daughter.'' His voice dropped to a seductive whisper. ''I want to marry her only because I love her.''

A sob caught in Seona's throat as she hugged him tightly. ''I...I wish we could leave here together this very night,'' she murmured.

''Seona,'' Griffydd said softly, holding her to him. ''I would prefer that, too, but it would not be prudent. Waiting will be difficult for both of us, yet I would rather delay a little while so that nothing can come between us.''

Her heart seemed to be tearing in two as she looked into his loving gray eyes.

Then she reached up to kiss him.

Tomorrow, she decided, tomorrow she would find the words to tell him that she could not marry him.

As for now, this one last time she would kiss him with all the love in her heart.

This one last time she would show him her true feelings.

This one last time she would be alone with him.

This one last time, she thought desperately, the sad refrain becoming an *iorram* in her mind.

He returned her kiss passionately. She allowed herself the pleasure of rejoicing in the feel of his hard, muscular body against hers. She caressed his back, stroking him from his shoulders to the tops of his breeches.

She should stop him, should end this here and now. She was promised to another, and the fate of her people might rest on that betrothal.

She felt his hands in her hair. Then he tugged out the lace binding the braid and ran his fingers through her loosened locks. His touch inflamed her even more as his hands traveled slowly downward, past her shoulders to cup her buttocks and press her close.

How she wanted Griffydd! Wanted his passion and the love in his eyes. Needed them, as a tree needs light and water.

She was going to be blighted soon enough, given in marriage to a man she did not love. Would never love as she loved the man who held her now.

Their kiss deepened, lips moving with sensuous necessity, tongues entwining in foreshadowing.

This one last time.

Was it so wrong to give in to the yearning she felt, to the passionate desire coursing through her body?

She might only have a short time before the trade negotiations were concluded. Then he would be gone. Gone forever. Never to be seen again. Touched again. Kissed again.

Like this one last time.

Leaning against him, she savored every particle of his body beneath her fingers, slowly caressing him.

He pulled back and drew in a great, ragged breath. "Seona, you must marry me. I need you. I want you for my wife, to bear my children. To be with me always."

She knew that could not be.

And then her *iorram* changed.

Chapter Fourteen

This one time, Seona's heart commanded.

Just this one time to be with him. This one time to love him, fully and completely. This one time to grasp a life's worth of happiness.

As for honor, did chattel have honor?

She stepped back and, without a word, drew off her belt. It fell to the ground as he stared at her with desire-darkened eyes. "Seona…?"

"Love me, Griffydd," she pleaded fervently. "Love me now. Tonight."

Before he could refuse, she drew off her gown and let it also fall to the floor. She stood naked before him, her only covering her unbound hair.

"We will be married," he promised as he reached out for her.

She smiled at this honorable man who would not take what she was offering without some kind of promise between them.

"I will always be yours," she replied softly, and truthfully, hoping it would be enough.

It had to be, for there was no more she could say.

"Seona!" He swept her into his arms and laid her on the narrow bed. In another brief instant, he had shed the *brat* and *chroich* and was beside her.

"I love you with all my heart, wife-to-be," he murmured, pressing featherlight kisses upon her forehead and cheeks. "I am yours forever."

"Shh," she hushed, afraid that if he called her "wife" again she would start to weep. "Later. We will speak of these things later."

Even though she knew full well that there could be no later for them.

All they would ever have was this one time.

Griffydd wanted to love her slowly, this first time. He wanted to enjoy every moment of their intimacy, to savor every touch and sigh and moan. He reveled in the feel of her naked flesh beneath his palm, and the sensation of her lips upon his.

He wanted to delight her in every conceivable way.

With that the only thought in his mind, his lips left hers to trail along the pulse of her neck, then lower.

His mouth captured her rosy nipple. Flicking his tongue delicately, he thrilled when she arched against him, her breathing fast and shallow.

Still he continued, moving lower.

She put her hands on either side of his head. "What—?" she gasped even as she shifted, instinctively parting her legs to give him more room. She murmured his name, sounding unsure and yet excited, too.

"Let me do this," he murmured gently. "Let me pleasure you, my love."

Her breath seemed to catch in her throat as he continued. Then, when he lifted his body over hers, her breathing grew more hoarse and her hips moved instinctively as he slowly entered her, her undulating movements exciting him, too.

No woman had ever aroused him so, or made him feel as if he were the most virile man in the world. As if every move he made was right and good and exciting.

He reached the point where he usually withdrew.

They were not formally wed or even betrothed. She might get with child—his child.

Instead of compelling him to stop, that idea filled him with even more desire for this woman who was his, who would always be his, as he was hers forever.

She was everything a woman should be, in every way, and it would make his happiness almost too complete to contemplate if she were to bear his child.

"Griffydd!" she cried out, arching and bucking in the throes of an ecstasy that matched his own, her pulsating muscles providing what little impetus he needed to reach the apex.

He growled with purely primitive release, then collapsed against her, breathing hard.

He realized she was crying.

Very gently he pulled away and lay beside her. "I'm sorry if I hurt you," he said with genuine remorse. "I fear I may have been too...hasty."

She brushed away the tear from her cheek and smiled tremulously. "You did not hurt me. That is not why I was crying."

He smiled with relief. "I have heard of women who cry at such a time."

Her brow furrowed for a moment. "Then that explains it."

"Seona," he said gravely, "you know a man of my age will have been with other women." He lifted her hand and kissed her fingertips. "But they are all forgotten now, and I will never want another. Only you."

She looked away from him with charming modesty. "If...if something were to happen to me, you would surely find someone to take my place."

He gently cupped her chin and turned her head to look into her eyes. "If something were to happen to you, there would be an empty place in my heart forever."

"Oh, Griffydd," she cried softly, clinging to him. "I love you, but I am not worthy of you!"

Griffydd DeLanyea, knight, son of the most powerful baron in Wales, more content and happier than he had ever been in his life, smiled indulgently.

"Of course you are," he said, stroking her hair. "I love you, Seona, and when you are my wife, I will make certain you never have such doubts again."

Seona's only response was a ragged sigh while she continued to hold to him tightly, as if she had fallen into the sea and he was come to save her.

"Olaf?"

"What is it?" the Norseman demanded. He recognized Diarmad's voice, but he was in no humor to be polite.

He had changed his clothes and washed, but his hair still stank of ale and his pride still smarted from Seona's impertinent act.

"It is Diarmad. I would speak with you."

"Very well," Olaf replied sullenly.

The chieftain entered his tent, and Olaf was glad to see that the man seemed properly subdued.

"I have come to ask your pardon again for my daughter's behavior."

"She shamed me in front of your warriors."

"My lord," Diarmad said, spreading his hand in a gesture of reconciliation, "I humbly beg your indulgence."

"Yet I am expected to marry a such an impertinent wench," Olaf muttered without looking at the older man as he tugged a comb through his thick hair. "I think I had best speak with Haakon first."

"We have clasped hands," Diarmad reminded him. "I have spoken with my daughter, and she is aware that she acted most improperly. It is only that she is a proud woman, as a jarl's wife should be."

Olaf gave Diarmad a shrewd, sidelong glance.

"Will she be willing to do what her husband commands of her?"

"Of course," Diarmad replied firmly.

"So you say."

"Are you telling me you wish to break our bargain?"

Olaf rose from his chair and stood before Diarmad. "If I did, and although her insolent behavior would be the reason, I am certain you would want compensation."

"I would deserve it," the chieftain replied.

Olaf scowled. "Then I will not break the bargain."

He came close enough to Diarmad that the older man could smell the reek of ale. "But you had best make sure she understands that I deserve respect. I will not take another such impudent act lightly—nor will Haakon."

Diarmad nodded. "I would expect no less of you, my lord. Trust me, Seona knows her place."

The Norseman's only response was a curt nod before he went back to combing his ale-soaked hair.

Diarmad went to the entrance of the tent. "I bid you good-night."

"And you," Olaf mumbled.

After a few moments, the tent flap parted again. Still far from mollified, Olaf frowned darkly when he saw who stood there.

"My lord, I am so sorry!" Lisid cried sympathetically.

He ran a cool gaze over the beautiful woman. "Perhaps you should return to your jealous husband."

An angry look crossed her face, followed by one of determination. "I do not want to go home, my lord."

"I did not ask you what you wanted," he replied.

She sauntered closer, the movement accentuating her sensuous grace. "Besides, Naoghas is in a drunken stupor, my lord. Snoring."

He began to feel aroused. He eyed her again, comparing her to the thin, insolent woman he was pledged to wed.

When Lisid had appeared before him that first night, he had truly felt as if a goddess had deigned to visit him, and when she had made the purpose of her visit clear, he had been almost too stunned to act upon it.

Almost. She had been incredible. He had questioned her afterward, for truly he had been too thrilled and excited to ask for an explanation before, and she had told him that she hated her husband. One look at *him,* she had said with an enticing shyness, and she could not prevent herself from wanting to be with him.

"And your children?" he asked as she ran her hands up his arms, her breasts in titillating proximity.

"Sleeping, too."

With a lustful grin, Olaf pulled her onto his lap, hushing Lisid's soft, throaty laughter with a fiery kiss.

* * *

Seona lay warm in Griffydd's arms, their bodies covered by his *brat*. For this time, between deep sleep and wakefulness, she allowed herself to drift on the edge of a dream.

A dream of being Sir Griffydd DeLanyea's wife.

She let herself forget that she was secretly promised to another, the bargain made and sealed. She would not recall that there was nothing she could do, unless she wanted to risk the wrath of the king of Norway falling on their village. On little Fionn and darling Beitiris.

The memory of Beitiris in Griffydd's arms filled Seona with another kind of bittersweet, searingly painful longing. How fine a father he would be! How much she wished she could be the mother of his children.

What if she were already with child?

The thought made her wide-awake.

If that happened, she decided, she would keep the knowledge to herself and press for an early wedding to Olaf after Griffydd DeLanyea had sailed home to Wales. She would hide the loss of her virginity, as well as the true identity of the child's father. That would be her special secret, to be kept and cherished.

Suddenly she wished she was with child. Then she would have something of Griffydd DeLanyea that would be hers forever.

He stirred beside her and she gazed at his handsome face, so grave and forbidding when he was awake, so relaxed and almost boyish in his sleep.

With cautious fingers, she delicately traced the outline of his strong, stubbled jaw.

She should wake him. He must not be found here with her, or seen leaving, either. If that happened, questions would be asked, answers demanded. Griffydd could learn of her betrothal.

How would he feel when he found out that she had led him to believe she was free to become his wife?

She knew full well how a man of his honorable character would feel—deceived and betrayed.

But she could not bear to send him away just yet. A little more time in his arms, that was all she wanted.

Fortunately for her, whatever happened, Griffydd could be trusted to keep their tryst a secret. He would not spitefully shame her even if he learned what she had done.

He had said he wanted to speak with his father first, and for that, she was grateful. She hoped he would learn of her betrothal before he was to return to Dunloch. That way, she would not have to see Griffydd's face when he found out what she had selfishly done.

She would not have to see the anger come to her honorable lover's eyes when he learned of her deceit. She would not have to destroy his love for her with her own words.

What would her father or Olaf do if they suspected Griffydd DeLanyea had taken her maidenhead?

Could the bargain not be broken then? Surely Olaf would not want a defiled wife.

Yet the fault would be hers. The blame would be

hers. If there was retaliation from Haakon, the cause would be her actions. Her selfishness. Her shame.

Griffydd stirred again, turning in her arms with a smile on his face and opening his eyes to look at her with such tenderness it made her heart ache anew.

"Seona," he whispered before kissing her passionately.

She nestled against him, then lifted his hand and kissed his palm. "You should leave, Griffydd," she said with genuine regret.

He slowly shook his head. "Not yet, my love," he sighed before pulling her to him for another fervent kiss.

It took all her effort to stop. "You must go, Griffydd, before you are discovered here," she said as firmly as she could.

She hated to see his boyish happiness fade, replaced by the stern warrior's resolute visage.

"I am not used to skulking about in the shadows," he remarked, sitting up and putting his feet on the floor so that his back was to her. "I am not a dishonorable rogue who takes his pleasure slyly. I would far rather declare our love to your father at once."

She put her arms around him and laid her head against his naked back, feeling his tense frustration. "I know, but you yourself said we should be cautious. As for any dishonor, it is my fault you are here, for I did not have the strength to send you away."

"No, Seona," he said grimly. "I did not have the strength to leave you."

"What's done is done, Griffydd, and I will have no regrets."

"Nor I," he said. He twisted to give her a wry look over his broad shoulder. "My foster brother maintains that secrecy increases his ardor. I must say, I think he's mad. But if we must be secretive, we must."

Then, sighing, he stood and looked around her little house as he drew on the *chroich*. "This is very neat and tidy, Seona. But it must have been lonely for you, too, living by yourself."

"It is," she confessed, hungrily savoring this near-domestic moment as a man might his last meal on earth.

"It *was*," he corrected. "You will never be lonely again, I promise you."

She was going to be more lonely than she had ever thought possible when he was gone.

Grinning, he glanced at her. "I fear I require your blanket, my lady."

Rising, she handed him the *brat* and reached for her own dress.

As he attempted to adjust the cloth, he said, "When you are my wife, I will see that you have the finest gowns."

She only nodded, then went to his aid. This time, she did not rush. She allowed her fingers to caress his taut, muscular torso.

"God's wounds, Seona, I do not want to leave you!" he whispered again, reaching for her.

Regretting and yet not regretting the ardor her actions had inspired, she deftly avoided his grasp.

"You cannot linger here," she reminded him.

He sighed ruefully. "And I used to pride myself on my self-command." He glanced down at his new garments. "I shudder to think what Dylan will say when I come home with these new clothes."

"He will be impressed, I'm sure."

Griffydd pulled her close. "Not nearly as impressed as when I bring home my wife," he murmured with another tender smile. "I do not want to go."

"Griffydd, the day will be long for me, too," she whispered.

"I will see you in the hall tonight, won't I?" he asked.

"Of course."

She embraced him, loving him, drawing strength from his presence, no matter how short-lived it must be.

"My family will surely come to care for you as I do." He chuckled softly. "Well, perhaps not so well as I," he amended. "But they will all respect you and make you welcome, of that I am sure."

"You…you had best get on your way," she stammered, stepping back.

"Very well," he said with obvious reluctance. "And have no fear. I have been trained by Urien Fitzroy himself, so if I cannot creep about a village without being seen, no one can."

She knew she had to let him go—and yet she could not accept her fate without protest, without action.

She was already mired in a terrible and shameful deception. What more harm could there be?

"There is one thing that will make the long day bearable," she said. "Will you come to me again tonight?"

She saw him grow tense.

"I know we are not formally betrothed, but can you doubt that I love you?" she pleaded, so desperate to be with him while he was in Dunloch, she would do almost anything.

"No, I do not doubt it," he whispered huskily, pressing his lips against her hair in a gesture of farewell, "and because we will be wed, I shall come to you tonight."

Reluctantly she let him pull away and go to the door.

He peered outside. "We are in luck. There is a mist this morning. Until tonight, my love."

Then, with a small smile, he silently slipped away.

Later that night, lying in the darkness of Seona's house, sweat slicked and spent, Griffydd put his arm about her to hold her against him.

"You might have given me time to say hello," he murmured wryly, for she had ambushed him the moment he entered the house.

They had been in the bed within moments, and making love only moments after that.

"I didn't want to waste an instant," she replied sorrowfully, nuzzling his neck.

"I am not annoyed. Indeed, I am flattered," he said, brushing back a strand of hair from her delicate face. "No woman has ever...attacked me...with such zeal."

"No?"

He laughed softly. "No. Trust me, I would remember."

Then his laughter grew more boisterous.

"What is it?" Seona inquired, raising herself on her elbow to look at him. "What amuses you so?"

"Dylan would not believe me if I told him."

Her brow furrowed and he realized he even loved the little wrinkles there. "Why not?" she asked.

"He claims I lack passion. I think I did, until you inspired it within me."

She laid back down. "Tell me about your family," she asked softly.

"Oh, Seona," he said with a sigh, caressing her lazily. "It is late and I am too tired. You will meet them soon enough."

"But I would know all about them before then. Please, Griffydd?"

He sighed again, but with patient forbearance. "What would you like to know?"

"Everything!" she said eagerly.

Almost hungrily, he thought vaguely. "That would take all night."

"I would willingly listen to you all night."

"But I must be rested to haggle with your father again tomorrow."

"Please, Griffydd!" she pleaded.

"Very well," he acquiesced, "but what I propose is this—I will tell you some of my family stories tonight, if you tell me some of your family stories tomorrow night. Then the next night, it will be my turn, and so on until either I've made an agreement with your father, or there is no more to tell."

"I fear my family stories will not be very entertaining," she murmured.

He lifted his shoulders to lightly kiss the tip of her nose. "If you do not want to tell me, I will not force you. I have seen enough to surmise that your life has been far more difficult than it should have been. Take heart, my dearest love! Those days are over now."

"Tell me about Dylan," she urged with a catch in her voice he did not hear as she lay beside him in the dark.

Chapter Fifteen

Just before the noon meal three days later, when all Diarmad's men were gathered in his hall, as well as Griffydd, Olaf and his crew, the chieftain rose from his chair. He waited until he had everyone's attention, including that of the serving women.

"Today I have made an agreement with Sir Griffydd DeLanyea," he announced, "who is here on behalf of his father, the Baron DeLanyea. In exchange for a fifth portion of the value of the trade goods, my men and ten of my ships will transport his silver and wool."

The warriors glanced at each other but, Griffydd concluded, they seemed more pleased than wary.

He kept a wry smile from his face as his gaze searched the hall for Seona. He saw his beloved watching from the corner and gave her a subtle wink.

The glorious, passionate nights they had spent together had confirmed his deep love for her, and hers for him, and his heart was full of happiness.

Perhaps he had been rather too magnanimous in his effort to conclude these negotiations quickly, so that he could get home to speak with his father regarding his marriage with Diarmad's daughter, but his father would consider a fifth part more than reasonable. He had authorized Griffydd to agree to up to a third portion of the profit.

Now Griffydd was anxious to return to Craig Fawr and confer with his father as to the best way to proceed. Then he would come back to Dunloch, where he would ask for Seona's hand in proper fashion, like the honorable knight he was.

While he understood the need for secrecy, he was deeply uncomfortable with the concealment of their relationship. Both of them were finding their subterfuge progressively harder to bear, too, especially Seona. During the past three days, she had grown quieter and more solemn when they were together, and she was not sleeping well.

Neither was he, for that matter, although between bargaining with Diarmad during the day and making love with Seona at night, he was as exhausted as he had ever been.

This situation had to come to an end, and so he had haggled less than he might have. Although Diarmad had groaned and complained, he—and now obviously his men, as well—were pleased with the outcome.

Unfortunately, this also meant he and Seona would have only one more night together before he departed.

He consoled himself with the thought that the next time he came to Dunloch, they would never be parted again. He would never again have to skulk about in the shadows and duck into her quarters like some disgraceful lout.

Diarmad spit in his hand and held it out to Griffydd.

"Now we seal the bargain," he declared.

Griffydd had been informed that this was the ultimate confirmation of a Gall-Gaidheal arrangement. Managing to keep his distaste from his face, he rose and likewise spit into his palm before clasping hands with the chieftain.

Diarmad grinned broadly, then lifted his drinking horn. "Let us drink to the trade pact I have made this day with the DeLanyeas of Craig Fawr!" he cried.

As Griffydd rose, he looked at Seona standing in the corner and smiled at her surreptitiously.

She did not meet his gaze.

Around Olaf, the rest of the men in the hall got to their feet. Still not quite sure what this trade pact presaged, the Norseman took a little longer joining in the salute, a delay that did not escape the note of wily old Diarmad, judging by the frown that creased his broad brow.

Still, the trade pact might be nothing more than a trade pact, Olaf thought. He himself was going to be the means for a more secure union between this clan of the Gall-Gaidheal and the Norse when he married skinny Seona, so he rose and drank.

"So, Griffydd, tomorrow you will return to Craig Fawr and tell your father what we have agreed on," Diarmad said as everyone returned to their seats.

"Yes. I think he will be pleased," the Welshman replied.

"He should be! A fifth—God's teeth, you are robbing me with my eyes wide-open!"

Grinning, Diarmad addressed Olaf. "Never have I had such an opponent. No arguing, just silence most of the time. God's holy rood, it is a rare man who can get the better of me, yet this one has!"

Slouching in his chair and with a less than enthusiastic smile, Olaf made another small salute with his drinking horn to the enigmatic Welshman.

That lucky foreign bastard was going to go back to his castle, while he had to stay and enjoy what passed for hospitality in Diarmad's village.

As he lifted his drinking horn for another gulp of ale, Olaf watched Seona move slowly about the hall, putting fresh bread before her father's warriors.

By Odin's beard, she was a homely, skinny creature! Her eyes were too big, her chin too pointy and her hair an abominable shade that only a witch should have. Perhaps her body wasn't bad, but who could tell for certain beneath that baggy, shapeless gown? Surely it would not be good enough to make up for her considerable faults, including her unacceptable impertinence.

She looked sickly, too. He had not noticed it at first, but as he had spent more time in Dunloch, he had started to notice the dark circles beneath her eyes. Her pale skin seemed almost translucent.

Maybe he would be lucky, and she would die soon after their marriage. Or maybe she was one of those thin women who looked ill and lived forever.

Unfortunately, she would probably always consider sharing his bed nothing more than her duty, experiencing no desire and giving no pleasure.

Not like the beautiful woman who truly stirred his passion.

He sighed wearily. He regretted that Lisid was not the chieftain's daughter. Of course, if that were true, Diarmad's daughter's dowry could be minuscule.

Yet what man in his right mind would care about that, if they got the beautiful Lisid, who was so accomplished a lover?

Olaf heaved another tired sigh and glanced at his host, who was busily stuffing his face with roast pig. Beyond him sat the Welshman, silently eating, his face betraying nothing of what was passing through his mind.

It was a pity Diarmad had not betrothed his daughter to the Welshman before he had arrived. Then he could have gone to his cousin and said, "Alas, Haakon, she is already promised."

Of course, he could easily imagine how upset his cousin would have been, and that Haakon would immediately have smelled a conspiracy that threatened him. Haakon always believed other men were plotting against him, watching for a moment of weakness, like wolves after a lone sheep.

Could a chieftain of a Gall-Gaidheal village and a Welsh baron whose land was far away really be a threat to Norsemen, though? Olaf mused, or was Haakon seeing potential peril that did not exist?

On the other hand, there were those longships of Diarmad's to consider.

Olaf smiled to himself when he thought of the shocked look on Diarmad's face when he mentioned his ships. Olaf and his crew had discovered them quite by accident when the lookout on the prow had called his attention to the odd formation of rocks on the shore.

When he married Diarmad's skinny daughter, Olaf reflected, perhaps he should tell the man to find a better place to hide his fleet.

Or maybe he should demand to have command of that fleet. That wasn't such an outrageous request for a son-in-law to make. Indeed, such a thing might almost make marriage to Seona an attractive proposition.

Olaf again watched Seona as she went out and returned with a large platter of meat, which she set before the old man sitting nearest the door. They spoke a few words and Olaf saw Seona smile.

She did have a pleasant smile. Then she put her hand to her back and straightened, arching as if to relieve an ache.

The movement made her gown tighten ever so slightly over her breasts and, with some surprise, Olaf realized they were very fine breasts, indeed. Perhaps if her arms had not been so thin and her features so unpleasing, he might have paid more attention to her other attributes.

He leaned back in his chair and meditatively stroked his beard. There might even be a passionate, lustful woman beneath that shapeless garment, who only required an expert lover to kindle her fire.

A man as expert as he.

To be sure, she was no Lisid. Lisid as mistress when he came to visit his wife's father, and Seona for a willing wife when he was home.

There could be worse fates than that.

Seona passed by the high table, ignoring him and her father, pausing a little before the Welshman as she set down a plate of bread. Watching out of the corner of his eye, Olaf saw DeLanyea reach for a piece, his hand touching Seona's.

And lingering there.

Not long, but too long not to raise a sudden suspicion in the Norseman's mind. Commanding himself to betray no sign, he raised his drinking horn, while his attention was focused on the Welshman and the chieftain's daughter.

They said no word, and in another moment, she had moved on about her business.

Surely it could not be, Olaf told himself as he glanced at DeLanyea.

Yet suddenly, Diarmad's request to keep the betrothal secret assumed a sinister cast. Why not tell everyone? If DeLanyea's mission was truly only to conclude a trade pact, why should he care if Seona was betrothed?

And a fifth part of the value of the goods being shipped—indeed, that was an excellent rate. Was any man that good a negotiator when his adversary was Diarmad MacMurdoch?

Thor's hammer, perhaps Haakon had been wiser than he thought. Perhaps this village chieftain had set his sights on an alliance with the Welsh and the Normans, too, if the Welsh were the DeLanyeas, and Seona was to be the means.

But Diarmad and he had formally agreed. That was a binding oath, as Diarmad would well know. If he had thought to make an alternate bargain with the Welshman, he would not have clasped hands with *him.*

Then what was he to make of this touch between DeLanyea and Seona? Could it be that they were acting in secret, making plans unknown to Diarmad?

Or perhaps, Olaf told himself, he was reading too much into one touch. After all, there had been no sign of anything between Seona and the Welshman prior to this single, simple act. Even now, Seona left the hall without so much as a glance at the high table. And tomorrow, DeLanyea would be gone.

Still…

*   *   *

Seona stood in the dark in the center of her little house, her heart aching. She thought she had known torturous moments of despair since she had been told she was betrothed to Olaf, but now when she had to tell Griffydd of her betrothal to another, she truly knew anguish.

It was to be kept a secret until the trade agreement was reached, and that had happened.

She could hope that her father and Olaf would wait until Griffydd had sailed before declaring her betrothal to Olaf, but she could not be sure they would.

Perhaps it would be a just punishment if he were finding out about her betrothal now, when she was not there to explain or defend her actions.

If she could explain or defend her deception to a man of his honorable nature.

Already tonight, Olaf had been different.

Even though they were betrothed, for the past three days he had seemed happy to ignore her, and Lisid, too, apparently. Tonight, however, she felt his gaze follow her as she went about her business.

She had been afraid to look at the high table, in case she caught his eye, and yet she was desperate to know what Griffydd might make of the Norseman's behavior.

As she waited, she tried to tell herself that whatever Griffydd thought, it didn't matter. In a short while, he would know that Olaf had every right to look at her.

Then tomorrow, Griffydd would be gone.

She went to the door of her house to peer into the

night, both hoping and dreading that he would be here soon.

She moaned softly as she went back inside. With trembling, cold fingers, she tried to light a lamp. Then she considered leaving her house in darkness. That way, when she told him the truth, she would not have to see his face. His eyes.

But that would be the coward's way. After what they had shared, she owed him that much—to look into his eyes and tell him the truth.

She had to try to find a way to make him understand her desperation, and that she had not been able to find the strength to tell him the truth before. Once he knew Olaf and her father had clasped hands and that the promise could not be broken, he would have refused to come near her, and she had not been able to accept that.

She hoped that he would remember that she loved him and the passion of the all-too-few nights they had shared.

The deception had not been easy for her. Every moment during their time together, hovering over her like an evil spirit, was the knowledge that as she lay in his arms, she was living a terrible lie, a sin of omission, for Griffydd still believed they would be married.

Once, lying awake in Griffydd's arms as he had slumbered, she had dared to consider that an alliance with the Welsh would be better for her people.

That had been but a momentary fantasy. Baron

DeLanyea had no ships to defend Dunloch if Haakon launched a vengeful attack, and his first loyalty lay to his own people, then the Normans. What would he be willing to risk for a village of Gall-Gaidheal? The wrath of Haakon on his people? The enmity of his own Norman king?

No. In her mind, she knew she could harbor no such foolish hopes.

Now, sitting on her bed, she laid her head on her knees and sighed with despair. What was she going to do?

Then she thought of Beitiris ripped from her mother's arms by one of Haakon's warriors, her brains dashed out on the cold ground. Fionn sold into slavery. Lisid beaten, raped and sold away from her children. The other women of the village sharing that horrible fate. Dunloch looted and burned.

Griffydd said he loved her. Maybe he would understand.

"Please, dear God, when I tell him, don't let him hate me!" she murmured, voicing her greatest fear in a fervent prayer.

The covering over her door moved and she rose, clasping her hands.

Then she stared as Olaf sauntered into her house.

Chapter Sixteen

"So, this is where you have gone to ground," Olaf said as he entered.

With his hands on his hips, his body seemed to fill her house completely as he slowly turned and surveyed his surroundings. "Small but neat, like on board a ship," he remarked, apparently impressed.

"What do you want?" Seona demanded, both annoyed and upset by his unexpected arrival.

"I thought I should speak with you," he said, stepping nearer to her.

Not wanting to be any closer to him than she already was, Seona moved back until the back of her legs struck her narrow bed. "Then speak or, as I would rather, leave at once."

"Surely there is no need for such a harsh tone," he said, spreading his arms wide in a gesture of supplication. "I am a guest of your father's."

"I know that," she replied warily. "And I also

know that it is unseemly of you to be here alone with me.''

"Your scruples prove you are an honorable woman,'' he answered, ''and I can appreciate that. But you have nothing to fear from me.'' He made a sardonic smile. ''Rather, it is I who should be afraid that you might pour something over my head.''

She could tell he thought he was being charming, but he was far too close for her comfort. ''You deserved that.''

"For making a joke?''

"For being rude. Now please leave!'' She pointed imperiously at the door.

He frowned. ''Perhaps you are forgetting who I am.''

"I know full well who and what you are,'' she said with a small measure of the scorn she felt, fighting not to reveal how she truly felt about this man she must marry.

"I think you should not be so unfriendly,'' he commanded, grabbing her by the shoulders and tugging her into his arms.

"After all, your father will not mind that I am here,'' he murmured hoarsely as he lowered his head to kiss her.

"But I do!'' Seona snapped, forcefully twisting free and glaring at Olaf, too angry now to care if she offended him or not. ''There will come a time when I have to submit to your embrace, but it is not yet come!''

His eyes narrowed. "So you know about the betrothal. I thought your father wasn't going to tell you."

"Then it would have been even more wrong for you to come here," she retorted.

He actually pouted. "I thought only to—"

"Seduce me? You could not wait for the wedding?" she demanded sarcastically. "You find me that attractive? I am flattered, my lord."

"I thought to make a peace with you," he declared.

"Go, then, or there will be no hope of that."

"I was thinking that it does not have to be so very bad."

"You do not want me. I do not want you."

"You could come to want me," he proposed. "I will make you a good husband."

She almost felt sorry for him then, because she knew that what he thought possible could never be.

"Perhaps," she replied, but her tone was not a hopeful one.

He regarded her sullenly. "I have as little choice in this as you, Seona," he said. "I have my orders, too."

"Shall we now talk of duty and honor and our responsibility to our people? Or perhaps we should speak of Lisid?"

He shrugged his huge shoulders. "If you would like. She offered herself and I took her. So what of that?"

Seona's lip curled. "Then go to her now, while you can."

"I will go to her whenever I like, whether I am married to you or not."

"So that is your idea of an honorable marriage? I am glad you have forewarned me. Very well, go to her. God knows we will be forced to spend enough time together in the years to come. Now I will take what solitude I can."

A new look came to his face. "You would send me into the arms of another woman? Why?"

"Why not? I do not love you."

Suddenly he looked like a warrior being challenged to do battle.

As she realized that she might have made him suspect there was another she cared for, he crossed the space between them and pulled her again into his unwelcome embrace. His mouth crushed hers in a hot, wet kiss and his hand fondled her roughly.

She shoved him away with all her might. "Get out!" she cried, pointing at the door. "And if you have any hope for happiness when we are wed, you will do as I say at once!"

"Seona," he growled, glaring at her and making no move to go. "You had best understand me. I am not used to taking orders, and I will never take orders from a woman."

"No, you are not used to it, are you?" she demanded angrily. "You are not used to being told what to do and when to do it. You are not used to being treated like a dog or a horse. Well, you are not my master yet. After we are married, then you can order me—not before. Now go!''

He didn't move. Instead, a sardonic smile spread over his bearded face. "Thor's hammer, you have spirit!''

"Get out!''

He slowly shook his head. "We are to be married, Seona," he said, "and by God, I am coming to believe it will be better than I thought.''

He took a step toward her. She snatched up a stick from beside the hearth. "Leave me alone!''

"Seona, Seona," Olaf murmured placatingly. "There is no need for this. Do you not see that I could enjoy having you for my wife? I should think you would be grateful. I am a jarl.''

"I will strike you if come closer!''

His low, deep, lustful chuckle seemed to fill the small building. Then he lunged for her, dragging her into his arms, forcing his lips over hers, stifling her very breath.

Desperate to escape, she flailed at him, the stick falling to the ground as she resorted to her bare fists.

To no avail, for he was taller, broader, stronger than she. Ignoring her struggles, he continued to kiss her as he dragged her backward. Toward her bed.

She cried out when he threw her down upon it, then scrambled away.

"Oh, no, you don't!" he cried, and laughter was

in his voice as he seized the back of her dress and yanked her to a stop.

She whirled around. "This is no game!"

He took hold of her shoulders, hurting her, his frigid blue eyes staring down at her.

"No, it isn't," he snarled. "This is a battle that I intend to win, woman. You can enjoy it, or not. It is up to you."

She spit in his face, then ducked her head to avoid the blow of his fist.

Which did not come, because Griffydd DeLanyea had grabbed Olaf's arm and, with savage force, was bending it behind the Norseman's back.

Enraged beyond any anger he had ever felt before, Griffydd continued to twist the arm of the man who dared to attack Seona.

But Olaf was a trained fighter, and bigger than Griffydd. With a roar like an angry bear, he shook himself free of the Welshman's grasp and shoved Griffydd back against the nearby wall. As he did, Olaf simultaneously drew a dagger and faced his opponent.

Griffydd crouched defensively. Seona saw, with increasing dismay, that he had no weapon.

"You nearly broke my arm, you Welsh bastard," Olaf growled. "I am the cousin of Haakon, fool. If you harm me, he will send a fleet against that one-eyed father of yours."

"I'm not going to hurt you," Griffydd replied

grimly. "I'm going to kill you for daring to touch her."

"He did me no harm!" Seona cried, fearful that one of them would be seriously injured or even killed, knowing that such a catastrophe would be on her head.

They paid her no heed.

Olaf lunged for Griffydd, who slipped past him, seizing the piece of wood Seona had dropped.

"Go, Seona!" Griffydd commanded, not taking his gaze from Olaf for a moment.

"No! Stop this!"

Distracted, Griffydd glanced at her, giving Olaf a brief opportunity to strike, which he didn't hesitate to use. He charged at Griffydd, who parried Olaf's up-raised dagger. The force of the Norseman's momentum was such that he crashed through the door, taking the covering with him.

Seona had a brief moment of hope that the fight would end, but Griffydd dashed after him.

"Griffydd, no!" she shouted, running outside into the darkness.

The moon shone through the scudding clouds, illuminating the two men grappling on the rocky ground. Griffydd was on top, his hands around Olaf's throat, while Olaf was likewise attempting to strangle the Welshman. Olaf's lip was cut and bleeding, a trickle of blood wetting his thick beard.

"Norsemen are all pirates," Griffydd charged through clenched teeth, his tunic torn at the shoulder.

"You only understand raping and pillaging and killing."

"And all the Welsh know is how to sing—and surrender!" Olaf snarled.

Seona didn't know what to do, or how to stop them.

"You'd better pray to whatever heathen god you will," Griffydd growled. "You are not fighting with a woman now, by God!"

"I have no need of help with the likes of you!"

Olaf succeeded in breaking Griffydd's hold and tried to roll away. Griffydd quickly tackled him again, landing on his opponent with a heavy thud. Olaf roared with anger and struggled like a fish in a net.

By now the sounds of the altercation had reached the nearest longhouses and a muttering crowd began to gather.

Now there could be no secret resolution to this, no quiet admission, no sorrow to be shared with Griffydd alone.

But no matter what happened, she vowed with wretched resolution, Griffydd would hear of her deception from no lips but hers.

She spied the piece of wood, also discarded beside them, and reached for it. "Stop!" she commanded, raising it high, her despair giving her the voice of authority as she prepared to strike even Griffydd, if need be.

Griffydd twisted to stare at her over his shoulder, and in that instant, Olaf managed to buck him off, sending Griffydd tumbling into the dirt as Olaf scrambled away.

Her father shoved his way through the crowd. "What is this?" he shouted.

He halted, arms akimbo, and took in the scene before him as the two men staggered to their feet. The chieftain's gaze darted from Olaf to Griffydd to Seona.

He finally addressed the panting combatants. "What is the meaning of this?"

"That man was attacking your daughter," Griffydd growled, glaring at Olaf with naked hate.

"I was not!"

Diarmad's eyes widened. "Are you two coming to blows over *Seona?*" he asked incredulously.

"Why not?" Seona demanded, coming to stand before him. "Why not me?"

He turned to face her, clearly taken aback.

"Not all men find me ugly," she replied, speaking with both frustration and despair. "Some can bear to look at me with favor. I can even be loved!"

Her father strode toward her, his nostrils flaring with anger. "What are you saying?"

What indeed? To what was she confessing?

"I am only saying that it is not inconceivable that a man could love me," she replied, keeping her gaze on her father's angry face, because she could not bring herself to look at Griffydd.

But her father could, and did. He glanced at Olaf, too.

"One man, or two?" he demanded of her. "And what do you mean by love? Have you been giving your favors to both?"

She did not answer.

"Are you your mother's daughter, after all? Did that whore taint you in the very womb?" he accused.

She flushed under his harsh scrutiny. "No!"

He raised his hand as if he would strike her, but Griffydd grabbed him as he had Olaf. Slowly he forced her father's fist downward.

"I will not allow you to strike a woman," he said, finally letting go.

She fastened her gaze on her lover, willing him to see her anguish, hoping he would understand. She confessed, her voice eerily calm now that the end of her brief interlude of happiness had come. "I am betrothed to Olaf."

Griffydd stared at her with shocked disbelief, for once his face showing fully how he felt.

"It is true," she confirmed softly.

His expression changed, to something hard and forbidding and terrible.

Then slowly he turned away from her.

"Your daughter is pledged to Olaf?" he asked of Diarmad in a voice that was as chilly as a sepulchre in winter.

"What is it to you?" Olaf demanded, feeling the cut on his lip. Then he paused, his eyes narrowing with wrathful suspicion as he glared at them. "Why did *you* come to Seona's quarters? If I have little right to do so, you have *none.*"

Diarmad frowned and scrutinized the Welshman. "After all your talk of honor and your duty as my guest, have you taken advantage of my daughter?"

Griffydd turned his cold gray eyes onto Seona. "Have I taken advantage of you, Seona?" he asked in a bloodless tone that made a shiver slide down her spine.

She shook her head. "No."

Diarmad still regarded him warily. "Are you telling me you have not had my daughter?"

"Do you always question your guests in such an insolent manner? Why not ask Seona for the truth?"

Diarmad considered a moment, then faced his daughter. "Have you been with this man?"

The gathering crowd fell silent around her.

What she said now could decide the fate of all here.

Griffydd regarded her steadily, his face an enigmatic mask.

Olaf stared at her, his eyes full of vindictive anger. Her father looked at her—and in his eyes, she saw something she had never seen before.

He was silently pleading with her.

The alliance with Olaf was so important he would beg of her with his eyes, if not words, not to destroy it. Finally, for once, *she* was important.

"I have never been with Griffydd DeLanyea."

With an aching heart, Seona looked at Griffydd, who did not so much as glance at her.

Why should he? She was a liar, a deceiver, an immoral woman. Surely she was less than nothing to him now.

Her father sighed with relief and the people began to whisper again.

Then Olaf turned toward the stone-faced Welshman. "Is that true?" he demanded.

Griffydd regarded him as a man might dung sticking to his boots. Slowly he advanced on the Norseman until the man retreated a step. "Do you doubt the word of your betrothed?" he asked in that same horrible, sepulchral tone.

Olaf shook his head. "No."

"When was this betrothal made?"

"Why?" Diarmad demanded. "It does not change our agreement. It cannot, for we have clasped hands on it."

"Yes, we have," Griffydd concurred. "But there was no need for any secrecy about your daughter's betrothal. It matters not to us if you make a strong alliance with Haakon."

"Good," Diarmad replied, relaxing a little.

"I wish to sail at first light, if that will be possible," Griffydd continued.

"Of course!" the chieftain answered.

Griffydd nodded once. "Good."

He turned his cold gaze back onto Olaf. "The next time you visit your betrothed," he remarked, "I suggest you be more quiet, lest another man think she does not welcome your presence. Now if you will all excuse me, I will retire.''

Still without one glance at Seona, he turned on his heel and marched away.

Out of her life forever.

No doubt silently cursing her and hating her.

''I am glad this was only a misunderstanding,'' Olaf observed, moving his bruised jaw. ''I would not like to have to meet that man in armed combat. Good night, Diarmad.'' He nodded at Seona.

He strode toward the Norse encampment, and she was glad to see the back of him.

She knew she would always be glad to see the back of him.

''It was but a mistake,'' her father declared to the crowd of muttering villagers. ''Go back to your homes!''

The crowd slowly dispersed.

Seona caught sight of Lisid among the onlookers. The woman's expression was distinctly hostile, but Seona didn't care. She didn't care what anyone thought of her anymore.

Before she could leave, her father took hold of her arm and pulled her close, so that his ale-soaked breath was hot on her ear. ''Were you telling the truth? Are you a virgin still?''

She looked at him, feeling nothing for him at all anymore, dead inside. ''Yes,'' she said, the lie coming easily. ''Were you telling the truth when you called my mother a whore?''

A strange expression passed over her father's moonlit face.

"She loved another and did not have the strength to give him up when her father made an advantageous match," he said bitterly before he walked off into the night.

Leaving Seona alone in the darkness.

While in the sight of the watchful villagers, Griffydd strode toward his quarters, his back straight and his head high like a valiant warrior marching into battle.

But by the time he was twenty paces from the threshold of his longhouse, everyone had returned to their homes to talk of what they had seen and heard, so there was no one to witness the slowing of his steps as he reached the empty building.

Nor did anyone see him stumble across the threshold as if he had received a mortal blow.

Chapter Seventeen

Baron Emryss DeLanyea threw himself in his oak chair beside the hearth in his hall at Craig Fawr and frowned petulantly at his wife. She glanced up from her embroidery to regard her one-eyed, gray-haired husband, then returned her attention to her work.

"I don't understand him," the baron muttered.

"Who?" Lady Roanna asked calmly, moving the frame a little closer to her knees.

"Your son."

"Yours, too," she remarked with the merest hint of a smile.

"More yours than mine when it comes to his silence," the baron replied. "God's wounds, he's been as quiet as a monk in a monastery since he got back from Dunloch, and it's been weeks."

"He's never been one for a lot of talk."

"Come, Roanna!" her husband cried. "You can't tell me you don't think he's quieter than usual, even for him."

Roanna put her needle in her work, then set the frame aside to look at her husband with her usual serenity, although there was also maternal concern in her eyes. "Yes, he is."

"Did he say anything to you about what happened there? All he told me is the terms of the trade agreement. A fifth of the value of the cargo and the use of ten ships is more than acceptable. I've assured him time and again I am pleased with the arrangement."

"Griffydd has said nothing to me of any difficulties, either," his wife said. She sighed softly. "I thought it best to wait until he wishes to tell us what is disturbing him. He has never been one to parade his troubles, and he is a grown man, you know, Emryss."

"Then you think something *is* worrying him?"

Roanna nodded. "Yes."

Emryss rubbed his scar beneath his eye patch. "If he doesn't say something soon, I will demand to know what happened in Dunloch!"

"Then he might never tell you."

"Well, I can't take much more of this moping about!" the baron declared. "He's like some kind of ghost."

"I have a guess as to the cause of his melancholy." His wife cocked her head to one side and regarded him with a little smile. "Tell me, my love, was there never a time you moped about?"

"No!"

"Not ever?" she pressed, a quizzical twinkle in her eyes.

A look of sudden understanding dawned on the baron's face. "You think he—?"

"Yes."

Emryss jumped to his feet. "God's wounds, why the devil doesn't he say there's a woman and bring her home? By God, he's no boy to be mooning over a girl! If he wants to marry, he should marry. Indeed, it's high time he did." He grew serious again when he saw his wife's face. "What's the matter?"

"If all were well, if the woman reciprocated his feelings and there was nothing to prevent a marriage, do you honestly think Griffydd would 'moon' over a woman?"

Emryss threw himself into his chair again. "You're right. Dylan would enjoy making himself miserable, but not Griffydd."

"Therefore," Roanna continued, "there must be an impediment."

"It cannot be Griffydd. Anybody would be proud to have him for a son-in-law!"

"There speaks a father," Roanna observed wryly, "and yet naturally I agree. Still, fathers are not always reasonable when it comes to their daughters."

"Then why does Griffydd not come to me? I could speak to the girl's—"

Roanna reached out to touch her impetuous husband gently on the arm. "If he does not ask for your help, do not interfere, Emryss. As difficult as it is, we must let Griffydd find his own way in this.''

The baron nodded and sighed, then got a familiar, determined gleam in his eye. ''One of the ships from Dunloch is due in a few days. When it arrives, I believe I shall make a few inquiries.''

''I don't think Griffydd would appreciate anyone prying into his affairs.''

''What prying?'' his father replied with an innocent and injured tone. ''I promise you, Roanna,'' he said, laying a hand to his chest, ''I shall be discretion itself.''

Seona stood near the ruined broch. The summer's day was a cool one. Overhead, a slate-gray sky threatened rain, and here on the bluff, a brisk wind stung her eyes and tore at her gown, making her light cloak billow behind her. She shivered, sick at heart and feeling ill.

In her hands, she held Griffydd's little Trojan horse, gently stroking its smooth surface as she looked out over the tempestuous sea.

This was where she had watched the ship bound for Wales sail away. Alone, keeping her gaze steadily upon the vessel, she had forced herself to witness the departure of the one man who had ever loved her, and whom she would ever love.

The man she had deceived.

But he had left the toy. When she had gone to tidy

Griffydd's quarters afterward, she had found it lying on the bed, as if deliberately left behind.

For her? Or Fionn?

Uncertain, she had picked it up—and known at once that whatever his intention, she could never bear to part with it.

It had been many days since then, yet the pain of her broken heart and lost love had not diminished. She feared it never would.

She glanced down at the sea below her, the waves crashing on the rocky shore. The white foam flew upward like arms reaching out to embrace her, only to fall back into the roiling sea.

If she fell to her death, what would happen then?

All her pain would be over.

Another wave of nausea assailed her and she put her hand over her stomach, guessing what blossomed there.

Despite the danger, she hoped she was right. She wanted to be right. She wanted her illness to be because she bore a child. *His* child.

A child to whom she would give the marvelous wooden horse and tell the tale of the Trojans and Greeks as Griffydd had told it to her. It would be a bond between them, even if she could never tell her baby where she got the toy or who had first told her the story.

Because of this child, she would live and find a way to survive, despite the desolate ache in her heart, in the hope that one day, the love for her baby would lessen her agony.

She heard a sound behind her and as she hid the wooden horse beneath her cloak, she turned to find Olaf watching her, a suspicious, quizzical look on his face.

She was going to be married to him in two days. Only two days.

"What are you doing here?" he demanded. "It is not safe to be so close to the edge of the cliff."

"I often come here to think," she said truthfully.

He glanced at the crumbling broch, then to the village. "You prefer to be alone?"

She forced herself to smile. "Yes, I like to be alone."

He held out his hand. "Come," he said not unkindly.

Without touching him, she moved toward him, away from the edge of the cliff.

"What do you want with me, my lord?" she asked.

Since Griffydd had gone, she had been the dutiful daughter and polite betrothed. Mercifully Olaf had made no further attempts to get near her beyond necessity, although he and her father had discussed the terms of the marriage agreement, the sum of her dowry and begun the preparations for her wedding.

She had accepted these things with resignation and a determination to do what she must for her people.

He studied her a moment. "He liked you, didn't

he?'' he asked dispassionately, without apparent jealousy or condemnation.

She knew who he meant. Ever since Griffydd had left her forever, she had noticed Olaf occasionally looking at her as if trying to decide if she had lied about their relationship. He would probably always suspect her of duplicity.

He might also suspect that the child she bore was the Welshman's, not his. Yet he would never be able to know for certain, for a baby could be conceived on a wedding night and arrive early.

Silently she repeated her resolute vow. She would never, ever let Olaf know for a certainty that she bore Griffydd's child. She would lie for the rest of her life about that, and she would keep her undiminishing love for Griffydd DeLanyea another secret, locked away in her heart until the day she died.

She could do it. Had she not deceived the man she loved? Was she not a master of deception now?

And if Olaf ever tried to condemn her child because of what he suspected *she* had done, she would stand between them with the fierceness of a mother bear protecting its cub.

Now, however, she didn't want to talk about Griffydd DeLanyea with anyone, let alone the man whose very existence made her marriage to the man she loved an impossibility. ''I don't know what you mean, my lord.''

''I speak of DeLanyea, of course. He came to your quarters that night.''

"He gave you an explanation," she countered evenly, grateful that Griffydd had deflected suspicion. He had done so without resorting to a lie, as she had done.

"I, um…" Olaf cleared his throat as if about to do something distasteful to him. "I ask your forgiveness for my hasty actions then."

"You have it." *And it has taken you long enough to ask for it.*

"Good. Seona," Olaf continued in a reasonable tone. "You don't care for me, and I don't care for you. We both know that. Why should we yoke ourselves unhappily to one another in marriage?"

"Because an agreement has been made that cannot honorably be broken."

He gave her a sly, sidelong glance that reminded her of Lisid, his lover. Still his lover, she didn't doubt. Nor did she care.

"If there was a way to break this betrothal, would you agree?" he asked.

She eyed him warily, trying not to feel any hope. She did not think she could bear more disappointment. "You have clasped hands with my father."

"That is so."

"Then the bargain *cannot* be honorably broken."

"I did not say it would be done honorably."

She stared at the Norseman, hating him more than ever. She had given up her chance for happiness rather than betray her father's word. "My people will be at risk if the betrothal is broken."

Olaf cleared his throat loudly and looked up at the sky. "Your selflessness does you great credit, Seona, but there is no need to martyr ourselves."

"If I don't marry you, Olaf, do you know what will happen to my village?" she demanded, gesturing at Dunloch. "Haakon might smell a betrayal, or conspiracy and vent his fearful wrath upon all here."

"He might," Olaf replied coolly. "What do the lives of a few peasants matter?"

It was all she could do to look at him now. "I will not have anyone suffer because of me," she said firmly.

Then she decided to put things in selfish terms so that he could comprehend. "No matter how you contrive to break the betrothal, my father will think it is my fault. I will suffer for it. Maybe he'll send me to a convent to live out my days in loneliness. Maybe he'll marry me to the next man who asks. Maybe he'll cast me out to fend for myself. Can you imagine my fate then?"

She went on before he could protest. "Olaf, a decision was made, and you helped to make it more than I. You, a jarl, could have protested. At least you would have been listened to. I had no such luxury. I was told it was done, and there was nothing I could do or say to change it. If I must live with that decision, why should you now be absolved? My father and your cousin want this alliance—and now so do I."

He stared at her in disbelief. "I will never love you."

"I know that. I will never love you."

"I could come to hate you," he snarled, telling her he already did.

"I do not care what you feel for me," she answered honestly. "I will have done my duty, and that will comfort me."

"You're mad! I offer you a way to change things, and you insist—"

She took a step toward him, regarding him with stern determination. "If I do not marry you, my happiness will have been destroyed for *nothing*."

"Maybe I should have let you throw yourself from the cliff," he whispered, his gaze held by hers.

"I was not going to do that, however tempting death would be compared to life as your wife," she answered. "There is the alliance to think of."

And her unborn child.

"You're a fool, Seona!"

"I have been called that many times, Olaf, but at least I will keep my father's pledge."

Olaf stared at her a moment with undisguised loathing, then shook his head and walked away.

Clutching the wooden horse to her chest, Seona turned back to look at the churning waters of the deep.

"Seona!"

Torn from her restless sleep, Seona opened her eyes

to see her father standing near her bed, glaring at her.

She glanced at the pillow beside her. The wooden horse was still out of sight beneath it.

"Yes, Father?" she asked, rubbing her eyes and wondering what had brought him here so early, and so angrily.

"What in the name of God have you done?" he demanded.

Clothed only in her shift, she sat up, pulling the covers over herself for warmth and out of some need to protect herself from his harsh gaze.

"I...I don't know what you mean," she stammered, suddenly fearful that he, or perhaps Olaf, had learned of her liaison with Griffydd DeLanyea and that she had been in the most intimate of embraces with a man she was not to marry.

"He's gone, damn him!"

"Who?"

"Olaf! Sailed off like a thief in the night, and taken that whore Lisid with him!"

"With Lisid? What of her children?"

"She's left them behind, like another slut I knew."

"I...I must go to them," she said, throwing back her coverings.

She remembered all too well the day her mother had abandoned her. The fear. The anguish. The tears. What she would have given then for a sympathetic face and a kind word!

"No, you won't," her father said. "Naoghas is fit

to spit splinters and he's raging like a mad bull. He vows to take his children and go to his mother's clan. He blames *me* for bringing on this disaster—me! As if I told Olaf to seduce his wife!''

''Fionn and Beitiris—?''

He scowled darkly. ''Are safe from his wrath. He loves them more than that whore ever did.''

''Then he is much to be admired, considering all that he has endured these past few years. Tell me, has he yet learned that Lisid had many lovers in Dunloch, yourself included?''

Her father gazed at her with shocked surprise. Then his brows lowered ominously. ''Forget Lisid, as he will! It is Olaf's act that is important!''

''He said nothing to you before he left?'' Seona asked. ''Gave no word, no hint of what he was about to do?''

She opened her mouth to tell her father of the recent conversation beside the broch, then thought better of it. Diarmad would surely chastise her for not coming to him immediately afterward, although Olaf had not told her exactly what he planned.

She had not given him the opportunity.

''How is it you saw nothing amiss?'' her father demanded. ''Did you not notice something between the two of them?''

''Nothing we all did not see,'' Seona replied. ''Why blame *me* if he has gone? I did nothing to cause this. *Nothing!*'' she insisted.

And he has left me with nothing. Absolutely nothing.

"Stupid, insolent girl!" her father snarled, grabbing her arm roughly. "Homely, foolish wench! Millstone around my neck. Useless creature!"

He shook her hard—then halted, staring at her.

She twisted away and put her hands protectively over her rounded stomach.

"Is that it, you whore?" he declared angrily. "He left because you bear another man's child? Whose?"

She raised her chin, not sorry that she bore Griffydd DeLanyea's child. For that, she would never be sorry. "What would you say if I told you the child was Olaf's?"

"Why would he sail off like a thief in the night if that were so?" he demanded skeptically.

"I have no idea. Perhaps he is in love with Lisid."

Diarmad sniffed derisively. "In love with that one? He is too clever for that."

"Perhaps he realized he did not wish to marry such a homely, skinny wench after all. You should not be surprised about that."

Diarmad studied her pensively. "He has fled without a word, so clearly he has broken his pledge. If you also bear his child…"

His expression altered, to a greedy one she knew well. "We will have to see that he pays for this, and well. Or his cousin the king will have to recompense, if Olaf cannot be found." Her father stroked his beard pensively. "This need not be a disaster. Olaf has acted most shamefully, seducing and abandoning you."

Then Diarmad grinned and Seona thought he was actually going to rub his hands together with greedy glee.

"So, no harm done and, indeed, some profit can be made," she said, taking no trouble to hide her disgust.

Which was just as quickly replaced with dismay. After giving up her hope of happiness, after making the man she loved hate her, after driving Griffydd away, she had been abandoned.

Again.

"What of me, Father?" she asked softly.

That made him frown. "I will think of something. There must be *somebody* who will marry you."

Seona straightened her shoulders and regarded him with defiant pride that would not be subdued, or shamed, ever again.

"I do not bear Olaf's child."

Chapter Eighteen

Enjoying the warmth of the afternoon sun and leaning against the armory wall of the castle of Craig Fawr, Dylan meditatively chewed on a piece of straw as he watched Griffydd battle the quintain.

The man had been swinging at the spinning dummy ever since breaking the fast, and Dylan was quite calmly wondering how long Griffydd could keep at it.

Dylan was not the only one, for several of the castle servants glanced curiously at the sword-wielding son of their lord as they went about their business. When they came through the courtyard again and saw him still swinging, they shook their heads in wonderment.

Finally, with the sweat dripping from his half-naked body, his damp hair plastered to his head and his shoulders slumped with exhaustion, Griffydd stopped to rest. Ignoring Dylan and everyone else nearby, he reached for a ladle of water from a nearby bucket, drinking some and pouring the rest over his head.

Dylan uncrossed his ankles and pushed himself away from the wall. He sauntered toward Griffydd, shaking his head, apparently with profound sadness.

"You are trying to kill yourself, then?" he proposed.

Griffydd reached for his tunic and wiped the back of his perspiring neck with it. "No."

Dylan took the straw from his mouth and tossed it aside. "Then what?"

Griffydd drew his tunic over his head and didn't respond, which wasn't unusual, even if it was frustrating.

"Your parents are worried about you," Dylan observed.

Griffydd's head popped out of the neck of his garment. "They shouldn't be."

"Well, they are. What happened in Dunloch?"

Griffydd reached for the ladle again. "Nothing that concerns anybody."

"Liar. Ever since you've come home, you've acted like you've got a burr up your backside."

Griffydd didn't even frown before he took a drink, while Dylan searched for something to say, hoping for a denunciation, at least.

"I know!" he cried. "It's a woman! The poor man is lovesick!"

Griffydd's eyes narrowed in a savage expression.

"Shut your mouth, Dylan, or I'll shut it for you!"

Griffydd growled, so fiercely that for the first time in his life, Dylan was actually afraid of him.

Too stunned to speak, Dylan could only stare as Griffydd grabbed his sword, turned on his heel and marched grimly across the courtyard and into the barracks.

Had he guessed aright? Was Griffydd upset over a woman? Had the sun stopped circling the earth, too, then?

Dylan glanced upward as if to assure himself that all of nature was not topsy-turvy.

What else would make a man act this way but love?

Dylan searched his memory for any woman Griffydd had paid particular attention to. There had been none in the days before he left for Dunloch. The last had been that Norman lord's daughter who had stayed at Craig Fawr over Christmas, and then Griffydd had only danced with her three times. Dylan didn't think he had even tried to kiss her.

Since his return from Dunloch, Griffydd had kept completely to himself. He rarely left the castle. He dined in the hall, then retired at once. He never accepted Dylan's offer to visit the village tavern, with their friendly and accommodating maidservants.

That left Griffydd's journey to the Gall-Gaidheal village, about which Griffydd had said nothing, save telling the baron the details of the trade agreement he had made with Diarmad MacMurdoch.

Dylan let out a low whistle. There must have been

a woman in Dunloch—and no ordinary woman, if she could make Griffydd this touchy.

Was Griffydd really lovesick? It seemed incredible, yet that explained his behavior.

Suddenly sure of his diagnosis, Dylan grinned. He would like to see the woman who could win grim Griffydd's heart.

A cry came from the watchtower. The port used by the fortress of Craig Fawr was some ways off, and that call meant that a ship had put in.

One of Diarmad MacMurdoch's was due any day, Dylan realized.

His grin changed to a cunning smile. He would make a little visit with the Gall-Gaidheal crew and see if he could learn something about Dunloch.

And the women who lived there.

Ignoring everyone, Griffydd strode into the barracks. He continued toward his bed, which was at the far end of the long, narrow room above the storerooms. Fortunately, all the men were elsewhere, either going about their duties, practicing their skills, or enjoying some sport.

He wanted to be alone. He didn't want to see the curious looks, the questioning eyes.

He threw his sword onto the bed, then stared at it, unseeing. If he really wanted his inner turmoil to be a secret, he would act as if nothing were the matter.

But he could not. For once, he could not hide his anger and his dismay, or his deep unhappiness that he had been deceived and lied to in actions if not with words and made to feel like the lowest, dishonorable cur who broke the bonds of hospitality to seduce his host's daughter.

That his pure love and honorable hopes had been polluted because Seona did not tell him she already belonged to another by her father's pledge, if not her own heart.

If she had, he would have kept himself away from her, no matter how difficult. He would have honored Diarmad's promise, if she would not, even when he knew she reciprocated his desire. His passion. His love.

He shoved aside his sword, then sat on the bed, his head in his hands.

Why must he feel this way for a woman he could never have? Why did he have to finally know what it was to love devotedly, only to discover that the woman he wanted was unattainable?

He blinked back hot tears that no man should ever shed, his sadness again threatening to overwhelm his control.

In his heart he knew that she was not alone in her guilt. He had been too weak and too cautious, thinking he should wait for his father's advice. He should have gone to Diarmad at once and asked for her hand.

Not having done so, a truly honorable man would have respected her and her honor, and waited until they were husband and wife to share her bed.

Seona had shown him that he was not as ethical

and pure and strong as he had believed himself to be, and for that, he should never want to see her again.

But he did. Every day, he thought of going back to Dunloch just for a glimpse of her face. Every moment was a struggle not to go to Diarmad to reveal the truth, and that he loved her still and wanted her for his wife.

But she belonged to another, he reminded himself.

Why had she deceived him? Only to share his bed? He was not so vain as to believe that.

Why else? He believed he knew: to distract him, so that he did not drive as hard a bargain as he could, just as he had suspected at the first.

God's wounds, he had been a fool! He had guessed what they were up to, and still fallen into their trap.

He should remember Diarmad and his daughter as prime examples of cunning, deceitful liars and villains who would do anything for profit.

Or so he told himself, over and over and over again.

Yet he found he could not drive Seona from his heart.

And so he suffered.

The baron, standing on the pier, glanced over his shoulder as Dylan dismounted and left his horse on the wharf.

"I thought you had no interest in commerce," the baron called to him. "What brings you here today?"

Dylan grinned as he came to stand beside him. "I

will be lord of my father's manor one day, so I decided it was time I started taking interest in matters of trade. Don't you agree?''

If Emryss thought there was something more to Dylan's unexpected arrival, he did not say so.

"That is a fine ship, is it not?'' he remarked instead, nodding at the vessel drawing closer.

"It is not the same as the others,'' Dylan observed, once again proving to the baron that Dylan had a shrewd eye for more than women. "The steering board is not on the right side.''

"No. This must be Diarmad's new ship,'' Emryss remarked. "Same crew, though,'' he finished wryly, running his gaze over the burly, bearded men who rowed the vessel closer.

About twenty feet from the wharf, the crew shipped their oars, leaving the ship to the control of the steersman as it glided in toward the pier.

The baron started and stared, not quite sure if he should trust his own eyesight or not.

"What is it?'' Dylan demanded. "Is something amiss?''

"I do not know,'' Emryss said quietly, his gaze not leaving the vessel. "I think that's Diarmad Mac-Murdoch himself in the stern. Why would he come?''

"Who's the woman with him?''

Emryss glanced at his farsighted foster son. "Woman?''

Dylan nodded, then turned to his uncle with a shrewd look. "A young woman.''

The baron's eye patch moved as he raised his eyebrow questioningly. "A young woman?"

"A young woman," Dylan confirmed. He gave the baron a questioning, sidelong glance. "I think I should fetch Griffydd."

If Dylan expected the baron to be surprised, he was disappointed.

"No, don't bring Griffydd here," the baron said evenly. "Have him wait in the hall—and don't tell him anything. Just say I want him to be there when I return."

Seona twisted her hands nervously as her gaze darted from her stern father to the castle in the distance, then to the man standing motionless on the wharf ahead. In addition to his one eye, the man's posture was so like Griffydd's, she knew he had to be his father, the Baron Emryss DeLanyea.

Now that she was here, so near Griffydd's home, she wished she wasn't. She wished she had not told her father that Griffydd was the father of her child. She wished she had kept the secret rather than face what could be a painful and public humiliation if Griffydd refused to see her.

She wished she had not thought to make one last, desperate attempt at happiness.

Surely she was right to feel this sense of foreboding. A man as honorable as Griffydd DeLanyea must hate her for her deception and involving him in that deception, whether she bore his child or not.

Perhaps even more for bearing his child out of wedlock, no matter what she heard of the Welsh opinion of such things.

If her father had any thought to force a marriage, Seona knew that would be hopeless. Griffydd, and surely his father, too, would never be coerced into something like that.

Neither would she. Not anymore.

Yet now here she was, terrified of meeting Griffydd under these circumstances, yet still feeling undeniable joy at the simple possibility of seeing his face again.

"DeLanyea!" her father bellowed, waving at the solitary figure.

The baron lifted his hand in acknowledgment as the ship docked. Besides his regal bearing, there were other attributes that told her he was no ordinary man.

First, there was the eye patch and the deep scar that snaked out from beneath it down his cheek. Then there was the man's thick, iron gray hair that hung to shoulders, which were broad and powerful despite his years. His cloak was thrown over one shoulder, revealing his sword—and the fact that the rest of his body seemed to defy the ravages of age, too.

This man was obviously a warrior to be reckoned with still. So Griffydd would be, too, when he was the same age.

But there was one great difference between father and son, and that was the welcoming smile on the baron's face.

As she pondered that dissimilarity, she realized that

the baron's smile had eased some of her trepidation, until she also realized that he would not know who she was, or why her father had brought her here.

Nervously she smoothed her new gown over her rounded stomach and tucked a stray lock of hair back into place.

Once the vessel had settled against the pier, Diarmad tugged her forward. She stumbled along the center of the ship, ignoring the scornful glances of the crew.

They had never paid attention to her before, or cared about her treatment in her father's household, so she would not worry what they thought. All her attention went to maintaining her balance, save for occasional surreptitious glances at the baron.

Diarmad disembarked, then held out his hand to help her but she nimbly—and independently— jumped onto the pier.

She raised her eyes to encounter the baron's searching gaze. Flushing under his scrutiny, she stared at the wood beneath her feet.

"Greetings, Diarmad!" the baron cried jovially. "I am delighted you could pay us a visit. And who is this fair lady?"

"This is no friendly sojourn," Diarmad replied grimly. "My daughter, Seona, has been disgraced by your son."

She risked another glance at the baron, whose face looked very grave—like Griffydd's—as he ran his gaze over her.

"Disgraced?" he asked calmly.

"Shamed. Ruined. Your son took her virginity and got her with child before he left Dunloch—and her already pledged to another!"

"Ah! Is this true?" he asked with surprising, and unexpected, gentleness.

She met his steadfast gaze and nodded slowly. "Yes. I bear his child."

"Do you doubt her word?" Diarmad demanded.

"Not at all."

"Has your son said nothing of what he did?"

The baron's lips jerked into a little smile. "He was always a quiet boy."

"Whether he told you or no, I will see that justice is done for my daughter and her child."

The baron held out his hands in a gesture of calming supplication. "Come, Diarmad! We are all friends here. Indeed, it sounds as if we are all relatives here. I am quite sure any misunderstandings can be made right at Craig Fawr. Let me escort you to my castle."

He gave Seona a warm and sympathetic look, something she had yet to see from her own father. "I am sure my wife will want to meet the mother of her grandchild. If you will excuse me, I will find a wagon to take you to Craig Fawr."

Seona watched the baron stride toward a group of men with horse-drawn wagons. He sounded so kind, and not the least upset.

She risked a glance at her father, whose expression was decidedly different.

"He acts as if nothing is amiss," Diarmad muttered, glowering. "He had better come to understand that it is!"

"Or maybe we should go home," Seona suggested.

Her father regarded her scornfully. "And get nothing for your shame?"

"You were convinced Olaf or Haakon would compensate you since Olaf broke the bargain. He abandoned me first, without knowing of my state," she reminded him. "Will that not content you?"

"DeLanyea owes us something, too. Your shame is no secret, after all. Olaf will likely claim now that he suspected you of immoral behavior and that is why he left."

"Without confronting us?"

"He will find some excuse for that, too," her father muttered.

Seona fell silent. It was futile trying to argue with him, just as she had known it would be hopeless to try to make him realize being brought here was more shameful to her than being with child out of wedlock in Dunloch.

The baron returned. A horse-drawn cart driven by a young man followed behind him, with another horse tied behind it.

"Diarmad, I will help Seona into the wagon," the baron said, untying the horse from the wagon and then leading it toward her father. "I am sure you would rather ride. This is not the best horse I've got, but I wasn't expecting such an important visitor. I'm sure you understand.''

With a grin lighting his scarred face, the baron waited for Diarmad to take hold of the reins, which he grudgingly did.

Then the baron took Seona's hand and led her to the wagon, where he put his hands about her waist and lifted her onto the seat.

''I trust you will not be overly uncomfortable,'' he remarked.

How like Griffydd's was his deep, melodious voice!

''No,'' she replied quietly.

''Good.'' Again the baron smiled. ''I confess I did not know my eldest son had such excellent taste in women.''

She made a small smile in return. ''He did not tell me his father was so charming.''

The baron chuckled softly, then went to his horse and mounted. He nudged the stallion to a walk and led the way toward the large stone edifice in the distance.

Chapter Nineteen

As Seona sat in the cart, she let her gaze rove the surrounding countryside. The hills were green and rounded compared to her home, and there were more trees. Birds sang in the woods covering the side of the valley and streams splashed into the nearby river.

It was a lovely place, lush compared to the rocky shore she was familiar with.

If only things had been different! If only she could have been traveling to this castle as Griffydd De-Lanyea's wife!

What would he think of her arrival today? More importantly, perhaps, what would he think when he saw that she was with child?

Would he be a little pleased to see her, or would he curse her to her face?

All too soon, and yet not soon enough, the little cart rumbled beneath the portcullis in the inner curtain wall of the imposing stone castle. She had not guessed that Griffydd's family was as wealthy or as powerful as this fortress implied.

As she looked about her, her father's initial command to keep Griffydd happy made more sense. Nor was it surprising that her father would want to make a trade alliance with such a rich baron.

These thoughts could not subvert her trepidation, however, which was not aided by the realization that a handsome young man, attired in fine clothes, was only pretending to check his saddle as he stood beside his horse at the entrance to the stable. His speculative regard made her blush anew, and realize this visit was going to be a trial in many ways, and not just where Griffydd was concerned.

Without a word, the young man went directly to the hall after a boy came to take the horses.

The baron gave the young man a rueful glance. "Pay no heed to Dylan," he said as he helped her gently from the wagon. "He's curious to see the woman who could win my son's regard, that's all."

Seona could scarcely breathe as she stared at the baron.

His regard? The baron thought she had Griffydd's regard? Did he know something she did not?

She fought to control her tumultuous feelings. Whatever Griffydd might have felt for her once, that was probably gone and she dare not hope otherwise.

A cherished child, he would never be able to understand the forces that compelled her to do what she did.

"Allow me to escort you inside," the baron said, holding out his arm gallantly.

She gratefully let him squire her toward the large hall.

Her father followed behind, still scowling, as they entered the huge hall. Fine tapestries hung on the walls and a fire blazed in the hearth.

Seona only noted these things with a small portion of her mind, for all her attention was claimed by the tall man standing beside an unknown woman.

Griffydd.

She wanted to run to him, to beg his forgiveness, to plead for his love—and yet she did not so much as meet his eye as she blushed with shame.

"Ah, my son!" the baron called as Griffydd approached them. "There is a lady here who claims an acquaintance with you."

Griffydd tried not to betray anything—not surprise, or joy, or shock, or dismay, even though all those emotions warred within him when he looked at her and saw the change to her body.

Seona bore his child!

Or somebody else's, perhaps. If she could keep her betrothal a secret from him, what else might she be capable of concealing?

"Yes, I know her," he said, trying to sound calm. "I am surprised to see her here."

"Know?" Diarmad bellowed. "That's a fine way to put it! You've got a child in her, you...you Welshman!"

"I thought she would be the wife of a jarl by now."

"*You* thought!" Diarmad snarled. "Hoped, more like, so that your betrayal of a host's trust would go undetected. I should run you through for what you've done!"

Griffydd's hand drifted toward his sword. "I don't think that would be wise, Diarmad. We are not in Dunloch now, but Wales."

"Come, come, men!" the baron protested placatingly. "I am sure this is all a misunderstanding."

"Misunderstanding?" Diarmad cried incredulously. "He's shamed my daughter. There's no misunderstanding that."

The serene woman who had been standing beside Griffydd came forward.

The baron addressed her. "Roanna, may I present Diarmad MacMurdoch, chieftain of Dunloch, and his daughter, Seona. Diarmad, Seona, this is my wife, Lady Roanna."

The baron's wife was tall for a woman and not overly pretty, yet there was something about her large eyes and the look in them that Seona found comforting. She also realized where Griffydd got his grave demeanor, for their expressions were mirrors of each other's.

As Lady Roanna bowed her head in acknowledgment, Seona suddenly wanted this woman to like her, or at least not hate her, as Griffydd obviously did. He had barely looked at her, and when he did...

She wished he would not, because what she saw in his face only confirmed her worst fears.

They should not have come!

"We are delighted to have you in our hall," Lady Roanna said in a kind, maternal voice.

His beefy hands on his hips, Diarmad swiftly bowed his head in the briefest of acknowledgments before speaking to the baron again. "This is no courtesy visit, my lord. Your son has dishonored my daughter, and I demand compensation."

"Compensation, is it?" the baron replied. "I suggest we all sit down if we're going to talk business."

He glanced at a maidservant hovering in another entrance, perhaps to the kitchen.

"We should have wine, too," he declared in a louder voice. He gestured at the chairs surrounding the hearth. "Please, Diarmad, sit."

"Emryss," Lady Roanna said softly, "must Griffydd and Seona be a part of this? Surely they would rather be alone."

It did not ease Seona's intense discomfort to see the look that passed over Griffydd's face at that suggestion.

"Mother," he began sternly.

"She's right," the baron interrupted with a tone of unexpected and unequivocal command that told Seona where Griffydd had learned to speak with authority. "Griffydd, take Seona to the garden."

Griffydd wanted very much to refuse, but he didn't want to disobey his father, or listen to Diarmad's complaints.

Telling himself that taking Seona to the garden was the lesser of two evils, he held out his arm to escort her there.

When she laid her hand upon his forearm, he commanded himself to ignore the thrill of her touch. Nor would he give in to his overwhelming desire to tell her how much he still loved her. Or that seeing her again instantly revived all the passion he felt for her. Indeed, it seemed to have grown a hundredfold, despite his efforts to forget her.

She had betrayed his trust, and that is what he would remember, he told himself as he led her outside the hall.

Did every servant and hireling in Craig Fawr have to be in the courtyard today? he wondered disgruntledly as he crossed the open space, aware of their curious scrutiny. No doubt Dylan had spread the news of these visitors all over the castle.

He began to walk a little faster, or the next thing he knew, his father's ancient nurse would come tottering out demanding to know what was happening.

How could he tell Mamaeth, when he didn't know himself?

Seona panted a little as she tried to match Griffydd's long, angry strides. She would have to ask him to slow down if he kept such a brisk pace.

Fortunately, he halted outside a gate in a stone wall. He opened it and led her into a lovely garden.

Roses of many hues, from the palest to the deepest red, climbed upon the stone walls. Other flowers grew in the beds beside the brick pathways, their delicate odors mingling with the roses in a very pleasant way.

Under other circumstances, she would have been delighted with her surroundings. Now, they only added to her sense of loss.

He pointed to a stone bench and she sat gratefully upon it, although it was as cold as Griffydd's manner.

He didn't sit beside her but stood a few paces away, seemingly engrossed in the roses.

"This is my mother's favorite place," he remarked after a long moment. "She likes to sit here in the evening when the weather is fine."

"It is very lovely," Seona replied softly. "Griffydd, I…"

Suddenly he whirled upon her. "Do you really bear my child?"

"You do not have to acknowledge it."

"How can I be sure it is mine?"

His question pained her like a slap. "You have to take my word."

"Your word?" he demanded skeptically.

She rose and faced him, clasping her hands together and raising her chin. "I was not honest with you about Olaf, Griffydd. Believe me, I know it. I knew it then, but I would do everything the same again for the brief time we had together."

A strange expression flickered across his face. "Where is Olaf now? Did he break the betrothal when he found out you were with another man's child?"

"He didn't know I was with child when he sailed away."

Griffydd blinked. "What do you mean, 'sailed away'?"

"I mean he sailed away five days ago without a word to anyone, and took Lisid with him."

"What of her children?"

"Left behind with their father. He has gone from Dunloch and taken them with him."

"Oh." His inscrutable expression revealed nothing of his feelings. "You will miss the children, I think."

"Very much."

"Then there will be no marriage?"

"Do not feel sorry for me, Griffydd," she said. She didn't keep her own disgust out of her voice as she made a bitter smile. "My father is convinced your father should pay for my shame and I am the evidence. Then he will go to Haakon and demand more compensation because Olaf broke the betrothal agreement. At last, I have some value to him."

Griffydd walked away and fingered the petals of one of the roses. "You should have been honest with me, Seona. You should have told me that you were already promised to another in marriage."

"I could not."

He glanced at her sharply. "Were you suddenly struck mute, that you could not?"

"No!" She faced him resolutely. "I could not marry you, so I did what I did because I knew it was my only chance to be loved. I wanted to be loved—and for once in my life, I *was* loved."

"Then you dishonored yourself and made me a part of that dishonor."

She grabbed his arms and forced him to look at her pleading yet defiant face. "Yes, I was selfish. I thought to take a moment's happiness with you. I would do it again. Can you not understand? Can you not conceive of my heartache when I learned I had to marry Olaf, or Haakon might think my father was plotting against him? I had no choice, no say in my own marriage, so I *chose* to be with you for the little time I could."

"What of me?" he retorted. "You gave no consideration to me in your selfishness. I thought you understood that I do not show my feelings easily, but that I do have them, and unlike some, I do not love lightly. Yet no matter how strong those feelings, I prize honor and duty and trust, too. I would not have lied to you, as you have done to me. I would not have dishonored myself, or you, as you have done, for the sake of a necessarily brief physical union. *You should have told me.*"

"If you had learned of my betrothal to Olaf, you would never have come near me again," she countered. "God help me, I was weak and selfish, because I couldn't bear that. If you cannot understand—"

She turned away abruptly, too upset to remain.

"Where are you going?" he demanded.

"I am leaving. This was wrong, and I am sorry. Know that I will raise your child as well as I can, Griffydd. You may see your offspring whenever you like if you come to Dunloch. Now I think I had best go to my father and tell him I will not stay here any longer. Goodbye."

Griffydd reached for her and pulled her to a stop. "Seona!"

He let go, but his gaze held her with an even stronger grip than his hand. "You would make the same decision again?"

She lifted her chin and regarded him steadily. "Yes, I would."

"Why?"

"Because..." Her defiance dissipated, to be replaced with sorrow. "Because I loved you."

His expression altered. "Loved? What do you feel for me now?"

She did not answer. Could not, because she could scarcely draw breath as she looked into his yearning eyes.

His gaze faltered and his voice dropped. "I did not want a moment's happiness. I wanted you for my wife."

"Only the knowledge that many might suffer if I did not keep my father's word made me deceive you," she said, her heart racing with a hope that would not be quelled because of what she saw in his grave gray eyes.

"You said you would not have come here if your father had not forced you," he reminded her gently. "If I am the true father of your child, why not?"

"I thought you must hate me now."

He slowly shook his head. "I could never hate you—and I did try, Seona," he confessed softly. "But I will love you until I die."

"Oh, Griffydd!" she gasped.

"Since your former betrothed has lost what he never deserved, dare I hope—"

"Yes! Yes!"

Happiness overwhelming her, she threw herself into his welcoming embrace—and discovered she was crying.

"Hush, now, hush," he crooned tenderly, holding her gently.

"Forgive me for deceiving you," she said, choking and sobbing and smiling all at the same time, scarcely daring to believe that he loved her still.

"Forgive *me* for being a proud, stubborn, overly cautious fool who tried to ignore his heart. I should have gone to your father at once, not waited." He drew back and smiled tenderly at her. "I shall have to amend my error, Seona. We must be married as soon as possible."

"Only...only because I bear your child?" she asked tentatively, suddenly fearful.

His smile grew and love shone from the depths of his eyes. "Only because I love you and my life will be empty without you. Nothing would make me happier than to have you for my wife. Say you will make me the most blessed man in the kingdom as soon as we can arrange it.''

Tremendous joy filled her as she smiled, gloriously happy and certain of his love. "I will!"

Laughing with pure bliss in a way she had never heard, he hugged her again—then kissed her with all the passion she remembered, dreamed of, yearned for.

"Promise me we will never be apart ever again!" he murmured.

Someone suddenly, and loudly, cleared his throat.

They swiftly moved apart, to see Diarmad standing at the garden gate with a rueful-looking Baron De-Lanyea beside him.

Griffydd's arm went around Seona's shoulders and she felt no trepidation. She would never be afraid of anything again, and her father could never hurt her again, because Griffydd loved her.

"Obviously, they have reached an understanding," the baron said, glancing at Diarmad, "My son, do you want to marry this young woman?"

"Right away, Father."

"Good, good. I was sure you would, so I've already agreed to a betrothal, and unlike some brash Norsemen, we DeLanyeas keep our promises."

Seona looked from the baron to her father. "You've…you've agreed?"

"Aye, and why not?" her father replied. "His son's already been poaching in my forest."

"Well, Diarmad, surely the *amobr* eases your suffering," the baron remarked casually.

"What is that?" Seona asked a broadly grinning Griffydd.

"A sort of reverse dowry," he explained, flushing a little as if he were embarrassed.

Her gaze darted between Griffydd and his father. "I don't understand."

"I think I'll let you tell her," the baron said to his son, "since you have made it necessary."

"It is, um, the payment for your maidenhead," Griffydd explained.

"And it is only fair I get it," Diarmad declared, folding his arms and looking as sulky as a little boy. "I will have to travel to Haakon's court when he hears of this marriage and convince him of my loyalty."

"Surely your gift to him of five hundred silver pieces will demonstrate your sincerity," the baron said.

"You are giving Haakon five hundred pieces of silver?" Seona asked her father incredulously.

"It's your dowry," her father replied. "And the baron's idea. Although we're not at fault for Olaf's base action, Haakon probably has some other relative he would propose for a marriage. This way, he should accept your marriage to a Welshman."

"So your father loses the dowry, but he gains an *amobr*," the baron concluded.

When her father smiled, Seona eyed him suspiciously. "How much is that?"

"What?" Diarmad asked, his smile disappearing.

"How much are you making them pay for my virginity?"

"None of your business, girl!"

"You are worth more than money to me," Griffydd said staunchly.

Seona persisted, looking to the baron. "I fear he is taking advantage of you, Baron DeLanyea."

"Oh, I know he is," the baron said with a jovial smile. "But if a sum of money insures my son's happiness, it is well spent." His gaze grew sympathetic. "Do not concern yourself, my dear. And as I said, we have already agreed, so there is nothing to be done anyway."

"Griffydd, I—" she began apologetically.

Griffydd put his fingers to her lips. "There is nothing to be done. They have agreed."

Then he bent close and whispered, "Whatever he has paid, it would not be more than he can afford."

Seona smiled at Griffydd, loving him. And his father, too, for helping to make her happiness possible.

She tore her gaze from Griffydd to address the baron. "Thank you," she said softly, and sincerely. She was surprised to see the man blush.

"The least I could do," the baron mumbled. Then he turned to Diarmad. "Come, I think a celebratory drink is in order."

Diarmad nodded and the two men departed, leaving

the young lovers alone to enjoy their newfound happiness.

Later that night during an impromptu feast to celebrate her eldest son's betrothal, Lady Roanna surveyed the hall. Fortunately, her husband's old nurse had finally decided to retire for the evening. Mamaeth had nearly driven Lady Roanna to distraction talking about Griffydd's impending marriage, but at last she was free to make certain all was well within her household.

Nearby, the baron regaled Diarmad MacMurdoch with tales of the Holy Land, as well as seeing that the man was kept quiet and content with copious amounts of wine.

Before the feast and while Seona had a few moments' rest, Roanna had shared a quiet conversation with Griffydd. During that talk, he had told her of Seona's life in Dunloch.

Lady Roanna's early years had not been happy or carefree, either, and she felt growing respect and sympathy for her future daughter-in-law. Although Diarmad's behavior troubled Lady Roanna greatly, he would soon be gone, with seven hundred pieces of silver and one hundred of gold. It was a large sum, to be sure, yet not so much when the young couple's happiness was at stake.

She caught sight of her quiet, usually grave eldest son, who had managed to maneuver his future wife into one of the darker corners of the hall. Apparently they seemed to find it necessary to conduct their conversation in a most intimate manner.

Lady Roanna stifled a smile. She wished their courtship had been smoother, yet had not her own been difficult, too? Adversity either strengthened a relationship or destroyed it, and it pleased her to think Griffydd's had withstood a test.

A glum Dylan slumped into the chair to Lady Roanna's left and sighed heavily.

"What is it?" she asked, subduing another smile at the despondent frown on her foster son's face.

"Do I look that ridiculous when I'm in love?"

"Ridiculous? Griffydd never looks ridiculous, and I've never seen you in love," Lady Roanna replied evenly.

That brought a shocked look to the young man's face. "I've been in love plenty of times."

She smiled indulgently. "Not like that," she said, nodding at the happy couple in the shadows. "One day, I hope you will be."

"And I hope the king understands that we're not up to something with the Gall-Gaidheal."

"Emryss will see to that. He plans to write to the king himself—after first sending word of this marriage to our many friends."

"Ah!" Dylan cried knowingly. "Our many and powerful friends."

"They will want to know our happy news," she replied innocently.

"I wonder how Griffydd will feel when he finds out how much it cost to make this marriage."

Lady Roanna frowned a little. "You won't say one word to him on the subject, Dylan," she commanded.

Because Dylan admired, respected and loved his foster mother, and because she could be more fearsome in her anger than the baron, he said, "If you bid me keep silent, I will."

"I do."

"She's not much to look at, though, is she?"

"Love is blind."

"God's wounds, I hope not!" Dylan said, his voice grave but his eyes dancing with mischief.

"You may discover otherwise."

"Perhaps," he said dismissively. "Now if you will pardon me, my lady, I suppose I should wish Griffydd every happiness."

He started to rise, but Lady Roanna held him back. "Later," she said quietly. "Let them be alone."

Then she got a mischievous twinkle in her eyes. "Someday, Dylan, when you fall truly and deeply in love, you will not want to be interrupted, either."

*   *   *   *   *